Celebrating Milestones

THE LIFE AND LEGACY OF
THE HARPETH HALL SCHOOL

Dedication

For their steadfast commitment to superior education for young women and for their unwavering support of the founding of Harpeth Hall, we dedicate *Celebrating Milestones: The Life and Legacy of The Harpeth Hall School* to the founding faculty and staff members:

Miss Vera Brooks
Miss Patty Chadwell
Mrs. Sophronia Eggleston
Miss Frances Ewing
Mrs. Lucie Fountain
Mrs. Martha Gregory
Miss Billie Kuykendall
Mrs. Lenora Litkenhous
Mrs. Ruth Mann
Miss Lucile McClean
Miss Ella Puryear Mims
Miss Penelope Mountfort
Mrs. Margaret (Pat) Ottarson
Mrs. Mary Rasmussen
Mrs. Susan S. Souby
Mrs. Madeline Terry
Miss Roberta Wikle
Miss Catharine Winnia

Celebrating Milestones

THE LIFE AND LEGACY OF
THE HARPETH HALL SCHOOL

Thank you to the many
Ward-Belmont and Harpeth Hall
alumnae who contributed their
special memories to this book.

A special thanks to
Gilbertine Moore (W-B '35) who,
through a donation, has generously
underwritten a portion of the
development of this book.

Additional thanks to the following:
Mr. and Mrs. James W. Perkins, Jr.
for their donation in honor of
Emily Perkins Zerfoss ('75);
Mr. and Mrs. Walter Hughey King
for their donation in honor of
Carmine King Jordan ('65) and
Sallie King Norton ('71);
Mr. James W. Hofstead for
his donation in memory of
Ellen Bowers Hofstead (W-B '34)
and in honor of
Edie Hofstead Cabaniss ('65).

We have made every attempt to verify
names, facts and figures. Please forgive any
inaccuracies or inconsistencies.

Designed and Manufactured by
Favorite Recipes® Press
an imprint of

FRP

P.O. Box 305142
Nashville, Tennessee 37203
1-800-358-0560

Managing Editor: Mary Cummings
Project Manager: Jane Hinshaw
Designers: David Malone, Jim Scott
Copy Editor: Elizabeth Miller
Production Design: Sara Anglin

First Printing: 2001

Celebrating Milestones

THE LIFE AND LEGACY OF THE HARPETH HALL SCHOOL

Published by: The Harpeth Hall School

Copyright ©: The Harpeth Hall School
3801 Hobbs Road, Nashville, TN 37215
615-297-9543

ISBN: 0-9709107-0-3

Editor: Heather Cochran ('79)

Photo Editor: Betsy Koonce Sottek ('75)

Milestone Celebration Co-chairs: Sarah Winn Nichols ('83)
Emily Perkins Zerfoss ('75)

Illustrations: Janetta Fleming Concepcion ('75)

Chapter Writers: The Heritage—Patty Delony ('66)
and Patty Litton Chadwell (W-B '35)
1950s—Beth Creighton Harwell ('55)
1960s—Ginger Osborn ('66)
1970s—Nicki Pendleton Wood ('79)
1980s—JoAnna Warnock Blauw ('83)
1990s—Lacey Galbraith ('95)
Behind The Scenes—Emily Cate Tidwell ('75)

Contributing Writers: Adell Crowe ('74)
*Carol Clark Elam ('66)
Polly Jordan Nichols ('53)
Elizabeth Wright Ralph ('77)
Cathy Cate Sullivan ('73)
Sue Fort White ('73)

Editorial Board: Patty Litton Chadwell (W-B '35)
Polly Jordan Nichols ('53)
Sarah Winn Nichols ('83)
Emily Perkins Zerfoss ('75)

Special Thanks: Ann Teaff, Head of School
Beth Boord, Director of Advancement
Andi Boklage Holbrook ('87), Milestones Celebrations Coordinator
Elizabeth King, Special Events Coordinator
Lynn McDonald, Director of Major Gifts
Sallie King Norton ('71), Director of Alumnae Relations
Dianne Buttrey Wild ('66), Director of Admissions

*Carol Clark Elam graciously and thoughtfully helped with the publication
of this book and served as chair of Harpeth Hall's board from 1998 until her untimely
death in December 2000. The school is deeply saddened by her loss and appreciates
her devotion and efforts on behalf of Harpeth Hall through the years.*

Preface

This book was written to commemorate the 50th anniversary of the founding of The Harpeth Hall School. A team of alumnae writers and editors was assembled who solicited input from the entire Ward-Belmont and Harpeth Hall alumnae base. Alumnae comments ranged from entries stating that being in Harpeth Hall's chemistry class fostered a desire to be a doctor to musings on the absurd concoctions made during lunch period. There was, however, a common thread woven through the vast majority of material we received. Harpeth Hall is not just a school—it is an experience, a heritage and a community. Most graduates feel that their years at Harpeth Hall allowed them to develop their own voice or a healthy self-awareness, and many assert that their educational experience there would become the most important in their lives.

As our team conducted interviews, read through stacks of comments and pored over archival material, we became more and more aware of the uniqueness of this shared experience. We came to realize the extent of the sacrifices made by those who had gone before us to provide us with this rich educational opportunity. We are grateful to the many people who had the vision and commitment to participate in the founding of Harpeth Hall when Ward-Belmont closed in 1951—the board of trustees, the parents, families and the first students.

Additionally, we owe undying gratitude and admiration for the eighteen original faculty and staff members. This dedicated group believed that superior education for young women, the core values developed at Ward-Belmont and its tradition of excellence must continue. Under the direction of the highly respected Susan S. Souby, the former director of the high school department of Ward-Belmont, these risk-takers took a step of faith and began Harpeth Hall with a clear vision of the outstanding education it would provide. They held fast to this belief even though they were given no contracts or assurance that they would be paid through that first year. Working with minimal facilities and limited resources, these women, all but one of whom stayed through the entire first decade, prepared the first graduating class for acceptance into some of the finest colleges across the country. As role models and educators, this first faculty had a profound and lasting influence on each and every student.

Introduction

Founded in 1951 in Nashville, Tennessee, The Harpeth Hall School has earned a reputation during the last 50 years as one of the South's finest educational institutions for young women. It has remained true to its mission statement, which reads, "Harpeth Hall, an independent college preparatory school for young women, offers a traditional curriculum designed to challenge each student to her highest intellectual and creative abilities. The School's program strives to develop in each young woman the skills, self-esteem and confidence for having a successful college experience and for meeting the challenges of the future. Harpeth Hall is committed to a single-gender environment wherein each student can be equipped, nourished and motivated to meet her potential for learning as well as for living."

Harpeth Hall's roots are firmly embedded in the traditions of Ward-Belmont, which itself was founded through the merger of Belmont College and Ward Seminary. The sudden demise of Ward-Belmont in 1951 rallied a group of concerned parents and faculty to lay the groundwork for the opening of Harpeth Hall. Its opening in the fall of 1951 was nothing short of a miracle and a testament to the hard work and dedication of these individuals.

This commemorative book hearkens the reader back to 1865 when Federal troops occupied Nashville, then a city of 15,000 citizens, following the end of the Civil War. Despite being located in a city in turmoil, Ward Seminary for Young Ladies opened on September 2, 1865, and became an immediate success. Decades later, on September 4, 1890, Belmont College opened with substantial fanfare as a new school for young ladies. These two institutions with similar purpose eventually merged to form Ward-Belmont in 1913.

The story of these schools unfolds as students and faculty in each decade share reminiscences about traditions, events, buildings and people that helped shape their lives. Biographies of leaders beginning with Susan S. Souby, the head of the high school department for Ward-Belmont who served as head of the newly founded Harpeth Hall, are included, as are profiles of dedicated faculty who have been involved with the school from its founding to the present.

Anecdotes and photos that capture the essence of the school as it grew from the former P. M. Estes estate to a resplendent 34-acre campus ready to take its student body well into the 21st century are the focal points of each decade chapter. It is the memory of each graduate that *Celebrating Milestones: The Life and Legacy of The Harpeth Hall School* honors and applauds.

Contents

1865–1951: *The Heritage*   8

The 1950s: *The Beginnings*   36

The 1960s: *Coming of Age*   60

The 1970s: *The Tides of Change*   80

The 1980s: *A Time of Promise*   98

The 1990s: *A New Identity*   118

Behind the Scenes   138

Appendix   154

Index   158

1865–1951

THE HERITAGE

The visions of the founders of Harpeth Hall, Ward-Belmont, Ward Seminary and Belmont College were consistent: each was to be an institution dedicated to providing excellent education to young women. Because the schools were founded many years apart, the lives students could expect to live after graduation were quite different. There are therefore vast differences in the course offerings, extracurricular activities and cultures of the schools. Many aspects of Ward-Belmont, founded early in the twentieth century, now seem quaint. Despite the superficial differences, Ward Seminary, Belmont College, Ward-Belmont and Harpeth Hall share many values. Most important among these values is a commitment to develop within each young woman the skills, self-esteem and confidence that will prepare her for life as a responsible and well-educated adult. It is therefore appropriate to begin the story of Harpeth Hall's first 50 years with the story of Ward-Belmont, which was established in 1913 through the merger of Ward Seminary and Belmont College.

Dr. W. E. Ward

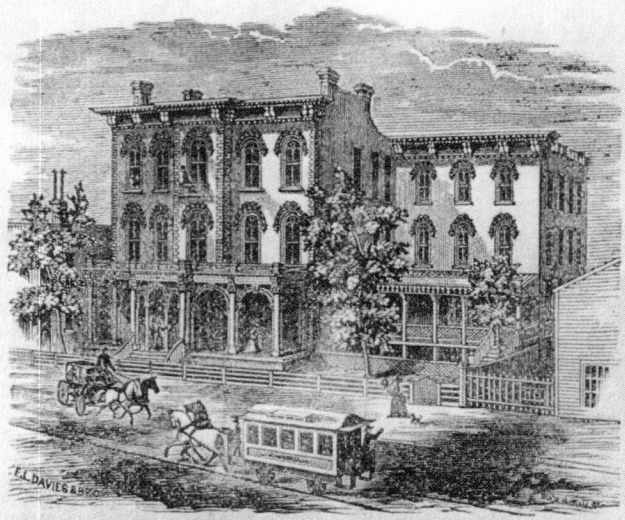

W. E. WARD'S SEMINARY FOR YOUNG LADIES is one of the noted institutions of the city. It has been in operation seven years, and has averaged about 300 pupils for four years past. It takes rank with the leading schools in the United States. The Building is magnificent in its proportions and architecture, and has all the late improvements. It has beautiful grounds, a graded yard for croquet, and a ten-pin alley for physical exercise. Its graduates rank high in scholarship, and many of them find good places as teachers. It was chartered in 1867. It is central to the city, and its pupils enjoy the best church advantages. Nashville is a beautiful and healthful situation for educational purposes. For catalogues and information, address

W. E. WARD,
NASHVILLE, TENN.

Ward Seminary

Ward Seminary for Young Ladies was founded in 1865 by Dr. William E. Ward and his wife, Eliza Hudson Ward. The term "seminary" did not then necessarily carry a religious connotation; in the case of Ward, it meant a school for higher learning. Ward offered "a full and thorough course of instruction, embracing academic and collegiate work." While grade levels were less specific than they are today, the courses offered and the ages of the students generally corresponded to the equivalent of high school and junior college.

Born in Alabama in 1829, Dr. Ward graduated from Cumberland College in Lebanon, Tennessee, and served as a minister of the Cumberland Presbyterian Church. It was the suggestion of his wife that he establish a school for girls in Nashville to fill the void created in 1863, when Federal troops forced Dr. William Elliott to move his famous Nashville Female Academy south to Montgomery, Alabama. Assisted by a loan from Mr. Byrd Douglas, Dr. and Mrs. Ward rented the Kirkman residence near the state Capitol at the corner of Summer Street (now Fifth Avenue) and Cedar Street. (It is an unusual coincidence that the Wards' landlords, the Kirkmans, were relatives of the family who later deeded Kirkman House to Harpeth Hall in 1986.)

On September 2, 1865, the Wards opened their school with 30 girls present. It was a time of turmoil in Nashville: the Civil War had ended just a few months earlier, but Union troops still occupied the city and controlled the destiny of its 15,000 citizens. Much lawlessness prevailed, and streets were not considered safe at night. The city was just beginning to emerge as a center of education: Montgomery Bell Academy opened two years later in 1867; Vanderbilt University was founded in 1873.

Ward Seminary was an immediate success. By March 1866, enrollment had increased so much that Dr. Ward purchased from Mr. W. P. Bryan a new site on Spruce Street (now Eighth Avenue). The Bryan residence was an ideal place for a school, with large rooms and a shaded tree-lined walkway in front of the house. As increased enrollment created a need for more space, surrounding buildings were annexed. The seminary also owned a farm where Baptist Hospital is now located; this was used for weekend recreation for the students and for long walks from Spruce Street in the afternoons.

Ward Seminary
1888 Graduating Class

Ward's motto *Mens sana in corpore sano*, "A sound mind in a sound body," indicates that athletics were an important part of the development of a Ward student. At first, the program of physical culture concentrated on dancing and calisthenics. As more active sports became proper for young ladies, athletic offerings expanded to include riding, bowling, roller skating, golf, tennis and swimming. Ward Seminary had the first girls' varsity basketball team in the South and one of the first in the nation.

Entertainment included Saturday night soirees in the formal drawing rooms, where girls entertained each other and the faculty with musical performances and recitations. After presenting a letter of introduction from a student's parents, a young man might take a girl on a Sunday afternoon ride on Nashville's new McGavock and Spruce Railway of mule-drawn cars. Occasionally there was an exciting event, such as President Hayes' goodwill visit to Nashville in 1877. The president was committed to the removal of Federal troops from the South, and Ward decorated for his visit with flags, bunting and hanging baskets of flowers. The president halted his carriage in front of the school to receive a silver tray of flowers from a student.

The school quickly developed a widespread reputation for quality education. In 1870 the Educational Bureau in Washington, D.C., ranked Ward Seminary among the top three educational institutions for young women in the nation. Course offerings included Latin, French, German, mathematics, science, expression, art, physical culture, home

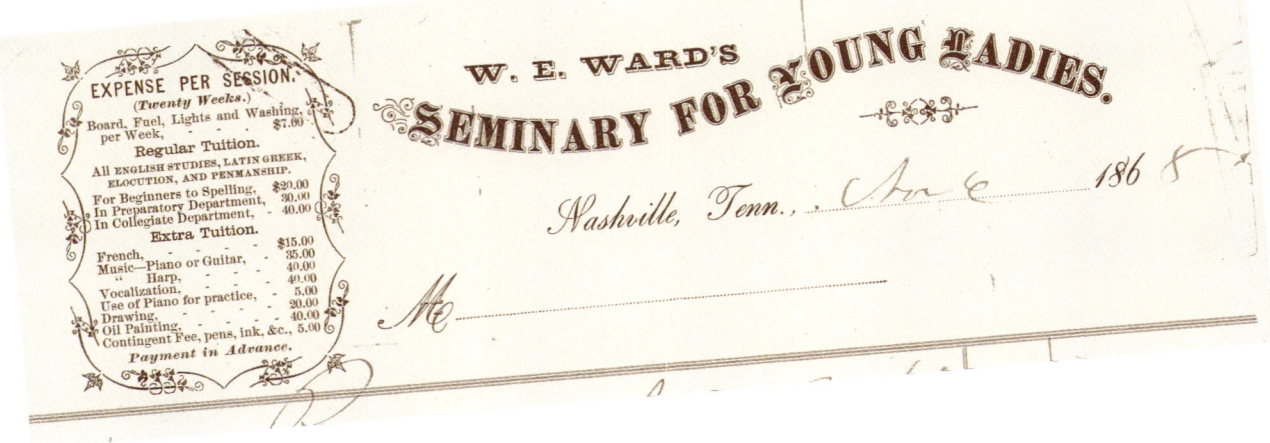

economics and domestic art. Faculty members held degrees from such prestigious institutions as Columbia University, Wellesley College, Smith College, Harvard University and the Sorbonne.

More than 3,000 girls attended classes at Ward Seminary during Dr. Ward's 22-year tenure as president. Dr. Ward's successors were Mr. J. B. Hancock, Rev. B. H. Charles and Mr. John Diell Blanton from Virginia, who served as president from 1892 until the school merged with Belmont in 1913. Mrs. Mary H. Robertson was principal of the school department throughout the administrations of Dr. Ward, Mr. Hancock and Dr. Charles.

In 1891, the seminary was purchased by the Presbyterian Cooperative Association of Nashville. Although owned by the church, it remained nonsectarian. By 1911, the school had outgrown its buildings on Spruce Street. There was a need to spend several hundred thousand dollars for new buildings, but there was no space on the campus for more structures.

Ward Seminary Tennis Team

Belmont College

Belmont College, founded by Misses Susan L. Heron and Ida E. Hood, opened in the former Acklen estate, Belmont, with substantial fanfare on September 4, 1890. The *Nashville Daily American* called the new school for young ladies "the Vassar of the South." The inaugural ceremony, filled with the pomp and circumstance befitting an institution of its stature, was indeed a grand occasion. The event was described as "a red letter day in the educational annals of the city."

The 1891 Prospectus of Belmont College for Young Women states that the school was modeled on the women's colleges of the Northeast, offering a "broad and scholarly education" while "obviating the necessity of leaving the traditions and institutions of the South during the formative period of young womanhood." As "the acknowledged centre of culture and education in the South," Nashville was an ideal location for such an institution. The designations of class levels in the Belmont College yearbooks, the *Iris,* are somewhat confusing, but the academic program appears to correspond to the years of high school and junior college.

Girls from prestigious families all across the South and Southwest filled the inaugural class, and 40 other girls had to enroll elsewhere. The *Daily American* said, "The roll call yesterday contained the names of ninety young ladies . . . daughters of the very best people of the sections they represent, and no more appropriate school-house could have been provided for them than this." The newspaper account described the campus in glowing terms, stating that the "grand old place" had never looked more beautiful, having had "every improvement that money and science can furnish." The school buildings combined the "stately grandeur of an ante-bellum mansion with the cosy conveniences of modern invention."

Miss Hood

Miss Heron

Belmont's Founders

Little is known of Belmont's founders, who were deliberately vague about their past lives. No record could be found of the schools they attended, their hometowns or family history. Miss Hood, a Quaker, probably grew up in the Philadelphia area. Miss Heron, a Presbyterian, may have been from Iowa, where the town of Ida Grove is said to have been

Acklen Hall in the late 1920s

named for her. The two met as classmates in Philadelphia and became great friends, announcing themselves to everyone as "Hood and Heron, or Heron and Hood."

A man who had known them in their early teaching years said, "Miss Heron was plump, redheaded, brown-eyed and evidently the leader." Miss Heron, described as strong-willed and "the embodiment of graciousness and dignity," took care of the school's business, while "the gentle Miss Hood," who loved poetry and was known for providing special encouragement to her students, had charge of the institution's academic side. Before coming to Nashville, the women had been co-principals of Martin College in Pulaski, Tennessee, for five years. They were considering a move to a larger city, perhaps Boston, in order to use their reputation for fine scholarship to better advantage. When they consulted Miss Heron's brother in Virginia about their plan to establish a school, he advised them to "Go South." Some friends in Nashville persuaded the ladies to consider the Acklen estate, Belmont, which was for sale following the death of its owner.

Miss Hood later wrote, "We were driving out Hillsboro Road when we saw it for the first time. Miss Heron was extravagantly pleased with the place and forthwith made arrangements for locating here." When friends later asked how they happened to choose the deserted Belmont estate, which needed extensive improvements to make it usable as a school, one of them would reply, "It was the old tower that did it."

NASHVILLE IN THE 1880s

Nashville had grown considerably in the 25 years since Ward was founded: the city had 76,000 residents and 9,000 students in 20 schools. The city's public transportation had just been converted from mule-drawn carts to electric street cars, which operated on 17 lines over more than 50 miles of track. The grand Union Station had been completed at the end of 1889, and workmen put the finishing touches on the train shed during the summer of 1890. A young man starting out in business could expect a salary of approximately $20 per month. A fine new brick house could be purchased for $4,500, with $800 down and the balance due at $38.50 per month.

The Belmont Campus

Belmont had been the home of Adelicia Hayes Acklen Cheatham, who developed the 640-acre estate with extensive parks and gardens, with her second husband, Joseph Acklen. The mansion was built in 1850 according to the blueprints of the internationally famous architect William Strickland of Philadelphia, whose other works in the area include the Tennessee State Capitol, Downtown Presbyterian Church and Belle Meade Mansion. Wooldridge's *History of Nashville* described the property as having its own waterworks fed by a limestone spring, a gas machine and appliances and an electric plant. The water tower, 105 feet high, was supplied by two fine springs. During the War Between the States, the tower served as a signal tower for Federal troops led by General Wood. The house and gardens were not molested, despite heavy fighting in the area.

Belmont class and teacher at the Bear House, originally part of the Belmont estate zoo

The 1889 purchase of the property by Misses Heron and Hood for $52,000 included the mansion, a brick bowling alley, pavilions, several greenhouses, the water tower and 15 acres of land. The ladies immediately began extensive renovation of the house and property. The structure known as Friendship Hall (later North Front) was added to the back of the mansion; other improvements included water and gas supply lines, sidewalks and an indoor swimming pool. The *Daily American* reported: "It is well known that more than $300,000 was spent on the house, grounds and outhouses, and doubtless much more if it could be investigated accurately."

Before long, the college had grown enough to require additional buildings. Fidelity and Founders Halls were added to the west and east of Friendship Hall to form the north facade of the campus. The three buildings looked down the hill (now 16th Avenue) toward the city of Nashville in the distance. The *Daily American* reported that the school was "connected with the city by a private street-car line."

A Strong Focus on Academics

Many of the founders' former students and several teachers came with the ladies from Pulaski to the new school. Other faculty were recruited from Wellesley College and Cornell University. Both Miss Heron and Miss Hood were determined that their school would be far more than a "finishing school." They stated that they believed in "girl brains" and felt that girls were "as deserving of development as boy brains." Accordingly, they instituted a rigorous academic program. The school's early cataloges stated that Latin and Greek were standard for Belmont students. Also included in the $60 per year tuition were class elocution, calisthenics and choral singing. Private lessons in piano and voice were available, each for $80 per year. Art and private elocution lessons were also offered. The 54-person Staff of Administration and Instruction in 1912 included a disciplinarian, two librarians, a postmistress, a nurse and seven hostesses.

Belmont's reputation for excellence attracted students from all over the country. In its final year, there were 376 students from 28 states. Most girls were from the South, but they came from as far away as North Dakota, New Mexico and Oregon.

Belmont College grew and flourished under the leadership of Misses Heron and Hood for 23 years. In 1913, the two ladies, "tired of school," decided to retire. They had built their dream home, Braeburn, at 211 Deer Park Drive in Belle Meade for $35,000, carefully designing the house with large reception rooms for entertaining friends and former students. [*Editor's Note:* This house is now owned by Vanderbilt University and serves as the chancellor's home.) The ladies are buried next to each other in the Mount Olivet Cemetery in Nashville, where their tombstone describes them as "friends eternally." Miss Hood died in 1921, Miss Heron in 1933.

LARGE ENROLLMENT

BELMONT COLLEGE OPENS UNDER AUSPICIOUS CONDITIONS.

WITH ENLARGED CAPACITY

New Building of Handsome Proportions and Superb Equipment Adds to the Advantages of the Institution—Pupils From Many States.

The opening registration of pupils at Belmont College Thursday morning was the largest in the history of the institution. The Regent and principals had not anticipated the contingency of having to turn away thirty young ladies with the additional accommodation provided. The capacity of the college is 225, and it is filled, and was so practically a month ago. All solicitation for pupils was stopped early in August, and for several weeks no additional registrations for the boarding department have been considered.

The student body, as seen in the chapel at the opening exercises on Thursday morning, was most attractive. The average age of the students is more advanced, and there is an air of earnestness of purpose manifest, both collectively and individually, that is very pleasing and encouraging.

It is an interesting fact that one girl in every five comes from north of the Ohio River. Four are from New York State, and four from South Dakota. Others are from Seattle, Portland, the City of Mexico, and every State from Minnesota to the Gulf and Florida. Many are from Ohio and Pennsylvania, and nearly a hundred come from Texas.

CUSTOMS AND REGULATIONS OF BELMONT COLLEGE (FROM AN EARLY CATALOG)

- Girls going out with gentlemen other than their own fathers must invite a chaperone. Gifts from gentlemen are not delivered, and flowers and candy are immediately sent to some charitable institution.

- Students are expected to keep an itemized account of expenses, and forward the same to parents monthly. Parents are requested to require this.

- Plans for daily exercise must be cheerfully met, the beautiful old Park of sixteen acres, the halls, veranda and balconies offering attractive inducements.

- Due reverence for the Sabbath prohibits visiting, reception of company, driving, unseemly reading, or loud and boisterous talking and laughing. Gossip, slang, exaggerations, fighting and frivolous conversations are deplored at all times.

- No student will leave the grounds without a chaperone, nor remain out of the College overnight except by special permission from parents and arrangement with faculty. Indolent and disorderly students must not expect visiting privileges.

- From first to last the student who wishes to be contented and successful must find her pleasure and happiness in study. Outside diversions may afford temporary relief, but they cannot compensate for the true happiness that comes with a sense of duty.

- Necessary shopping will be done by the College shoppers. A seamstress will come to the house when absolutely needed, not otherwise. All sewing and dressmaking, dentistry, photography, etc., should receive attention at home, since they seriously interfere with study and progress.

- Deliberate carelessness in regard to health is severely reprimanded; hence young women must dress properly, must avoid exposure, and articles of food must not be kept in rooms to be eaten at unseasonable hours. Light weight, long-sleeved underwear, heavier hosiery and high shoes are required in winter.

- All mail, packages, boxes and telegrams to and from the College pass through the hands of the management, subject to their inspection. Suspected communications are opened in the presence of the student or are immediately forwarded to parents, who are expected to select and limit their daughters' correspondents.

- Gentlemen callers must bring letters of introduction, but will only be received occasionally, and from eight to nine at night. Frequent and regular calling is not permitted. New acquaintances must not expect the privilege. Brothers may call on their sisters at seven o'clock Sunday nights.

- As room decorations each young lady will be allowed only four framed pictures, two photographs and two College pennants on her walls and dresser at the same time. Considerations of health and good taste necessitate this rule, which is inflexibly kept. A just regard for College property and for students who occupy the rooms afterwards should be a sufficient incentive to keep the custom cheerfully.

Establishment of Ward-Belmont

On September 25, 1913, Ward-Belmont opened, uniting Ward Seminary for Young Ladies and Belmont College for Young Women. The new school had a junior college, a preparatory school, a primary school and a music conservatory.

At the time Belmont's founders were making the decision to retire, Ward Seminary was looking for more space in a suburban location. With well over 300 students each, both Ward and Belmont needed new academic buildings and dormitories. While Belmont had extensive grounds, Ward had no available space for expansion. Commenting on the 1913 merger of the two rival schools, Louise Davis wrote in *The Tennessean:* "That the two schools of such similar purpose

should be joined, linked under the name Ward-Belmont, taking the buildings of one and the president of the other, seemed the logical answer to the problems of both."

Dr. Ira Landrith, who had served as assistant to Misses Heron and Hood, became Ward-Belmont's first president. Dr. John Diell Blanton, who had been director of Ward Seminary, served initially as vice president and chairman of faculty; he became president when Dr. Landrith retired in 1914. He served as president until his death in 1933, when he was succeeded by Dr. John W. Barton. In 1936, Andrew Bell Benedict became president. He was followed in 1940 by Dr. Joseph E. Burk, who had been dean of the school. Dr. Robert Calhoun Provine, former dean of faculty of Ward-Belmont, was elected the school's sixth president on June 6, 1945.

Choir 1948

Continuing the Academic Tradition

Ward-Belmont was noted for excellence in academics and music. In the first academic year, course offerings included English, history, mathematics, science, Greek, Latin, French, German, Spanish, psychology, education, sociology, expression, physical education, art, secretarial work, domestic science and a wide variety of music courses. The faculty and administrative staff of 62 held degrees from Vanderbilt, Yale, Northwestern, Wellesley, Columbia and other respected universities and colleges, and almost all the language and music teachers had studied in Europe. Students were "influenced to excellence by the likes of [teachers] Gertrude Casebier, Martha Ordway, Linda Rhea, Florence Boyer, Catherine Morrison, Susan Souby, Mary Elizabeth Cayce and countless others who cared," writes Jean Burk Bennett (W-B '39).

Belmont College for Young Women, 1890-1913

Continuing the tradition of academic excellence established by its predecessor institutions, Ward-Belmont in 1922 became the first junior college in the South to receive full accreditation by the Southern Association of Colleges and Secondary Schools. This was due in large part to the record of the alumnae, 93 percent of whom had graduated from universities after completing their two years at Ward-Belmont Junior College. At one time, a diploma from Ward-Belmont carried with it a certificate of privilege for admission to Vassar, Wellesley, Smith, Vanderbilt or the University of Chicago.

The Conservatory of Music in 1938 became the first junior college conservatory to be accepted by the National Association of Schools of Music. The College and Preparatory School were members of the Southern Association of Colleges and Secondary Schools throughout their existence; the College was also a member of the American Association of Junior Colleges. The School of Art held a chapter membership in the American Federation of Arts.

A brochure from the 1940s outlines the varied courses of study: "A majority of the students elect to take one of the more strictly academic programs composed of English, foreign languages, science, mathematics, history and the social sciences, psychology and philosophy. Others take special work in art, speech, home economics, secretarial training, or physical education. Some combine music with the regular college program and receive a certificate in piano, voice, violin, organ or harp along with their General Diploma. Still others, who intend to continue their studies on a professional basis, give their full time to the Conservatory program."

Describing the school to prospective students and their parents, the brochure states, "Ward-Belmont is not a large, cold impersonal institution with students of widely varying ages, outlooks, and backgrounds. The students are carefully selected, and the faculty and staff are chosen because of their fitness for the particular type of leadership and instruction that the school fosters. Emphasis is placed on *actual teaching*—not research. While predominantly Southern, students and faculty are a cosmopolitan group and come from some thirty-eight states and ten foreign countries. Everything on the campus—from beautiful Acklen Hall to the playing fields and unique Club Village—has been carefully planned for girls. There are unlimited opportunities for pleasant companionship at a most impressionable age. Girls live, work and play together simply and naturally.

"By means of regular hours, distractions are kept at a minimum. When work is in order, every student is expected to devote herself wholeheartedly to her studies. When studies are done, every student has ample opportunity to participate in the numerous extra-curricular activities, special interest groups and sports."

WARD-BELMONT REGULATIONS FOR DAY STUDENTS (FROM THE 1938-39 HANDBOOK)

Discipline

- A reprimand is a severe reproof.
- Suspension is the temporary severing of a student's connection with the institution.
- Expulsion is permanent dismissal from the institution. Any student who leaves the campus without permission, or who cheats in examination, renders herself liable to summary dismissal.
- A student who is found to be out of sympathy with the spirit and ideals of the school may be asked to withdraw even though she may not have broken any formal rules of the school.

Regulations

- Rouge and lipstick must not be used during school or gymnasium schedules.
- Chewing gum will not be permitted.
- Day Students must be dressed simply and in good taste.
- No Day Student may absent herself from assembly or club without permission from the Supervisor of Class Attendance.
- High School students may not sit upon the campus during study periods. College students may sit upon the campus in small groups.
- It is expected that College students use the library during the periods when they do not have scheduled appointments.
- Students may not sit on the stairways or in cars upon or adjacent to the campus. They must not loiter in the cloak rooms.
- Students must not deface the school property. Undue noise is not permitted in academic halls. Silence must be maintained in the library and in the study hall.
- Day Students must not meet young men upon the campus, nor are they expected to meet them adjacent to the campus.
- Day Students must not carry mail or telegrams to or from boarding students.
- High school students may not smoke on or adjacent to the campus, nor at any place during the school day.
- College students during the school day may smoke only on the campus in the room provided for that purpose.

The Little School

When Ward-Belmont was established, the school began with the primary grades so that the students of Ward Seminary's grammar school classes could continue their schooling without interruption. The Little School, as it was called, was always quite small with four to eight students in each grade, and teachers were often in charge of two grades. The first through eighth grades were discontinued one class at a time; the last class began first grade in 1931.

Miss Annie C. Allison closed her popular preparatory school for girls in 1923 and came to Ward-Belmont as head of The Little School in 1924. She also taught Latin. In 1925, she was installed as principal of the high school, a position she held for 20 years. She was succeeded in that post by Susan S. Souby. "Miss Annie Allison was the first friend I made at Ward-Belmont. It was November 1943 and I was entering as a high school junior after attending schools in Virginia, Georgia, Kansas and Arkansas during the previous four years. Her gracious manner and warm welcome made me feel safe and appreciated during those last three years of World War II," recalls Evelyn Dickenson Swensson (W-B '45).

Miss Annie C. Allison

The Ward-Belmont Campus

The 1919 yearbook described the campus in glowing terms: "There is nothing about Ward-Belmont that is not dignified and beautiful. Consistent with her lofty ideals and the admirable grace with which she does everything are Ward-Belmont's buildings and campus, which contribute their large share toward the unequaled atmosphere of the place."

The main buildings were grouped around a spacious quadrangle with one open side. On the north side was Acklen Hall, the mansion of the original Belmont estate (also known as Rec Hall). This was flanked by Fidelity and Founders Halls complete with drawing rooms, an auditorium and dining rooms. On the east side were three residence halls: Pembroke, Hail and Heron, where most prep boarding students lived. The John Diell Blanton Academic Building (known as Big Ac) and the gymnasium were on the south side of the quadrangle. The Conservatory of Music was in a building of its own with numerous practice rooms, two pipe organs, a music library with recordings, biographies, works on theory and practice of music, miniature scores and ensemble works.

In 1929, a 23-bell cast bronze carillon was installed in the historic water tower. The alumnae association and the class of 1928 gave the bells in memory of those who lost their lives in World War I. The bells rang on special occasions, and each new school year they welcomed the "belles" back to the campus. Every Christmas Eve, the community heard the bells as the school gave its musical Christmas card to the city.

Life at Ward-Belmont

Music and other cultural activities were a vital part of life at Ward-Belmont. The orchestra, glee club and string ensemble enjoyed enthusiastic support, and there were frequent lectures and performances by professional musicians. Members of the conservatory staff sponsored numerous vocal and instrumental ensembles and other music groups including the glee club, choir, Chamber Music Society and the Captivators, a student-directed orchestra that played popular music. Performances were sometimes given in conjunction with nearby boys' schools; Gilbert and Sullivan operettas were among the favorites. The Dean of the Conservatory, Alan Irwin, had an impact on many students' lives. "He was my piano teacher, my choir director at Belmont Church, where he invited me to sing in the adult choir, and my conductor of operettas by Gilbert and Sullivan at Ward-Belmont. By 1949 I was a piano teacher, choir director and a conductor of Gilbert

and Sullivan operettas for the DuPont Chorus in Waynesboro, Virginia, using all the skills he taught me," adds Evelyn Dickenson Swensson (W-B '45).

Literary organizations included the Wordsmiths for college students and Penstaff for preparatory students interested in creative writing. Students edited a yearbook, *Milestones* (a name that remains today as Harpeth Hall's yearbook); a weekly newspaper, the *Hyphen* (named in honor of the merger to form Ward-Belmont); and a monthly literary magazine, the *Chimes*. Other clubs for special interest groups included the YWCA, art club, French, Spanish and mathematics clubs, riding and athletic clubs.

There were no uniforms at Ward-Belmont, but there were very specific dress requirements. In the 1930s, for classes the girls wore shirts and skirts, flat shoes and absolutely no make-up. When they left the campus for shopping or other events in town, they were required to wear solid black, brown or navy blue dresses with matching hats and white gloves. For dinner each evening they wore dresses appropriate for church or street wear. In the early years, the gym uniform consisted of long navy blue serge bloomers worn with long black stockings and white middy blouses with navy ties.

MISS CATHERINE E. MORRISON

Memories of a place or an experience are almost always shaped by the people we remember. One individual that every Ward-Belmont student remembers is Miss Catherine Morrison, who taught physical education throughout Ward-Belmont's 37 years and served as athletic director from 1932 until the school closed in 1951. Her own memory was legendary: she knew every girl's name by the end of the first week of school. Even more amazing, when she was almost 100 years old, Miss Morrison could make a specific comment about almost every girl who attended Ward-Belmont during her tenure at the school. One graduate recalled being in a hotel lobby in Paris with her husband when Miss Morrison walked through, trailed by a group of Ward-Belmont girls, and greeted her calmly, "Good morning, Ann Caroline," as if there were nothing unusual about meeting many years and thousands of miles away from Ward-Belmont.

Catherine Elwyn Morrison, a native of Boston, began her career at Ward Seminary, where she was hired in 1910 as a physical education teacher. Since an instructor already at the school was able to handle the modest physical education program, Miss Morrison initially served as a chaperone, a substitute French teacher and the sponsor of the Christian Association. When the other physical education teacher left about a year later, Miss Morrison began to organize sports and other activities, including a May Day performance. She also arranged for the girls to take swimming lessons at the YWCA.

Two years later, Miss Morrison joined the newly merged Ward-Belmont as assistant to Miss Emma I. Sisson from Providence, Rhode Island, in the physical education department. These two New England women became fast friends, and together started a girls' camp—Camp Cohechee—in Fryeburg, Maine, on Lake Kezar, a beautiful spot where Ward-Belmont girls from all over the country spent many happy summers. The horses from the Ward-Belmont stables went to Camp Cohechee, too, transported back and forth by boxcar.

When Miss Sisson was made dean of women at Ward-Belmont, Miss Morrison became the director of the physical education department. A remarkable organizer, Miss Morrison supervised swimming, hockey, basketball, bowling, archery, tennis, golf and softball, as well as dancing and the equestrian program. She was a strict disciplinarian whose stern reprimands—especially those involving chewing gum or unruly shirttails—were remembered by all. Nonetheless, her "girls" knew that she was absolutely dedicated to helping them develop their abilities, and many of them stayed in touch with her long after graduating.

In the last years before her death in 1987 at the age of 101, she was blind and in a nursing home, but her mind and her wit were as sharp as ever. One day, as she lay in darkness in her bed, she demanded her whistle, put it around her neck, and exclaimed, "To think, when I would blow this whistle, 800 Ward-Belmont girls would come to attention." [*Editor's Note:* Miss Morrison's original whistle is now displayed in the Ward-Belmont room in Souby Hall on the campus of Harpeth Hall.]

Beginning in 1933, girls wore navy blue wool shorts, a white shirt and tennis shoes for gym classes. The 1945 specifications for graduation dresses, sent in a letter to parents from Miss Annie Allison, principal of the preparatory department, were very precise: "A long white dress of organdy, net, mousseline de soie, dotted swiss, eyelet pique, or marquisette, with some sleeves, and back not lower than eight inches below

the neck line. This dress need not be expensive, as an elaborate one would be very inappropriate."

Meals were served by waiters to round tables of eight in the dining room; each table had a teacher as hostess. Each boarding student was assigned to a table, where she was required to eat breakfast and lunch for three weeks at a time; at the evening meal, girls could eat wherever they desired. Menus were planned according to a rotating schedule; girls could count on ham, potato salad and cinnamon rolls for lunch on Wednesday. Day students, of course, ate only lunch at school, usually in the tea room (known as Tea Hole) in the basement of Pembroke Hall. Ward-Belmont alumnae have fond memories of tasty meals that included special favorites such as fresh fruit salad with cheese balls for lunch; roast turkey and dressing on festive days; and freshly-baked sweet rolls, gingerbread and rolls with cherry preserves. One alumna recalls

gaining 10 pounds during her first semester, and the little cookbook *Ward-Belmont Specials* was in great demand.

On Sundays, church attendance was compulsory; girls could attend any church of their choice but had to be accompanied by at least one other girl. Vesper services, usually led by the girls, were held on Sunday evenings, outdoors when weather permitted.

Most of the social life and athletic competition took place among the clubs, ten for boarding students and four for day students. After a rushing period in the first weeks of school, every student became a member of a club. The names of the boarding students' clubs—Agora, Del Vers, AK, FF, Osiron, Penta Tau, Anti Pandora, XL, Tri K, and TCC—are somewhat mysterious, and their significance seems to have been forgotten. Clubs sponsored teas, dances, open houses, day trips, volunteer activities, skits and other entertainments. Each club fielded a team in every sport, and competing for academic and citizenship awards were important elements of club life. The 10 club houses that made up Club Village were clustered around the famous old tower at the south end of the campus. Each house had a spacious living room with a large open fireplace, a music room, a game room, balcony and kitchen, and was fully equipped for activities and entertaining.

Sports were popular at Ward-Belmont; a catalog states that many girls who had never enjoyed athletics became so enthusiastic that their schedules included more than the required hours. The fall season opened with tennis and hockey, followed by basketball, bowling and posture classes in the winter. Spring sports included baseball, golf, track, tennis and archery. Dancing, riding and swimming were popular throughout the year. The physical education building had a gymnasium, a dance studio, bowling alleys and a swimming pool. One requirement for graduation was to be able to swim the length of the pool. Outdoor activities took place on two athletic fields, tennis courts and a riding ring. The school owned a stable of horses and offered instruction in horsemanship and road rides. "My favorite place was the stables and the riding ring . . . I had always ridden western style being from Texas, but Miss Carling taught me Eastern Equitation. I must have been pretty good because she sent me to show 'Little Jack' in a Nashville Horse Show and allowed me to ride in a real fox hunt across the beautiful Tennessee countryside," remembers Emily Lou Phillips Whitridge (W-B '32).

Dr. Leotus "Leo" Morrison (W-B '46) adds, "The philosophy of the department of physical education was influential in my thinking and I remembered the example of good, healthy competition and the educational potentials of that competition. I later went on to help develop sports opportunities, nationwide and in the Olympics, was president of AIAW—the group which started organized intercollegiate competition—and was involved in the development of local, regional and conference sports organizations."

The lives of day students and boarding students were necessarily quite different. The four clubs for day students—Angkor, Ariston, Triad and Eccowasin—had no houses but met in the clubhouses of the boarding students. They also had fewer events, since these girls had ample opportunities for social lives away from the campus with their families and friends. There were even separate student governments for day and boarding students, since their rules and penalties were somewhat different. Everyone had classes together, of course, and day students had the opportunity to make friends with boarding students during classes and athletic competitions.

Social events in all the clubs were for girls only, even dances, for which invitations were issued to members of the other clubs. Girls danced with one another, often with difficulty deciding who would lead. Only once a year were boys invited to a dance at Ward-Belmont; this was a formal affair for all students and was held in the dining room.

Clubhouse

"BEHIND THE IRON CURTAIN"

Local ladies who were considered to be suitable role models and to have good judgment served as "hostesses" or official chaperones for Ward-Belmont girls, and of course chaperones were required for train trips to and from school. These ladies, though remembered by the girls as rather severe, were not necessarily without humor. Sometimes a boarding student who was suspended from school for some infraction stayed with a chaperone for the period of her suspension if she lived too far away to go home. On one such occasion, when a girl was suspended for kissing a boy in the train station, the chaperone with whom she boarded felt that the punishment was excessive. Asked what she would have done if she had been on duty when the unsuitable display of affection occurred, the chaperone answered, "I wouldn't have seen it!"

An article written by alumnae Sarah Bryan Benedict ('31), Sarah Ophelia Colley Cannon (Minnie Pearl) ('32) and Mary Elizabeth Cayce ('26) described arranging for a date on the cloistered campus as similar "in process to getting behind the iron curtain." After a girl's family provided written permission for her to see a certain young gentleman, the home department issued a pink permission slip to the girl. The gentleman called at Acklen Hall and gave his name to the distinguished butler, Whitaker, who invited the caller in with pomp and dignity, reported his arrival to the home department and summoned the young lady to the reception rooms. According to the authors, "One wonders if this procedure was worth a two-hour visit in a Victorian parlor equipped with full-length mirrors at strategic points, hard horse-hair sofas, and a gliding chaperone who somehow floated through the rooms continually making her presence known by clearing her throat!"

Boarding students could not leave the campus without permission from both home and school authorities. When they did leave campus, it was in groups, almost always with chaperones. Rules were relaxed in the 1930s to permit girls to go into town on the streetcar, provided there were at least two girls together. Previously, trips to town were permitted only in taxis and only with a chaperone; girls tried to persuade their favorite teachers to go along as chaperones. "I remember leaving campus on Saturdays, complete with white gloves, and riding in the rain in cabs. After an afternoon of shopping downtown the last place we went was to Candyland for a luscious chocolate soda or sundae dripping with thick marshmallow sauce on chocolate ice cream," says Mary Ireland Fishback (W-B '39). Nashville residents easily recognized Ward-Belmont girls, who were well-known for their highly respectable attire and impeccable manners.

Special Events at Ward-Belmont

Holidays were celebrated in fine style. The traditional Thanksgiving dinner included roast turkey, chestnut dressing, cranberry sauce, candied yams, Brussels sprouts and plum pudding. A Halloween dinner featured such delicacies as Forbidden Fruit, Ancestors' Eyeballs, Frozen Faces, Ghosts' Sticks and Satan's Delight. Each month there was a formal birthday dinner served on special birthday china for all girls celebrating birthdays that month. A highlight of the year was the Christmas party with an exuberant program presented by the servants. A fund collected by the girls and matched by the school was divided among the servants. To express their appreciation for the gift, the servants put on a program the night before school adjourned for Christmas vacation. After dinner, the performing group came on stage in their white aprons and black uniforms, with "Cook" in his chef's hat. Together they would sing and recite a program of Christmas joy. The stars were always "Willie the Baker" Blackman, master of ceremonies, and Maggie Majors, a dorm maid who recited "Curfew Shall Not Ring Tonight."

May Day 1935

The annual George Washington Birthday Celebration was another special event at Ward-Belmont in which students assumed the roles of Colonial dames and gentlemen, dancing the minuet for "George" and "Martha." [*See* Chapter Two.]

Perhaps the most elaborate ceremony was the annual coronation of the May Queen, which took place on the lawn of the main quadrangle. Heralds announced the coming of the procession, led by girls bearing maypoles, which they placed at one side of the court. Bright streamers made a colorful background for the court dancers, who entered in procession. Everyone danced except the seniors, who entered last, gowned as ladies of the court. They formed a row on either side of the path leading to the throne to await the coming of the queen. The queen arrived in a horse-drawn carriage, attended by the College Maid and the Prep Maid. All students except seniors took one class a week in dance or directed exercise; the May Day program was a demonstration of the dance classes. In addition to the traditional Maypole Dance, dances included ballet, waltz, country reel and marching.

May Day 1942

An especially exciting event was the visit of President and Mrs. Roosevelt to the Ward-Belmont campus on November 17, 1934. Classes were suspended, and all the students, from the elementary school to the seniors, lined up single file around the circle, all dressed in white. Mary Lalla Byrn Turner (W-B '35), who was a senior, recalls being told to stand next to the girls with whom she would be most proud to be seen by the president. As the presidential party entered the campus, the bells of the alumnae

May Day Procession

carillon played "Hail to the Chief." It was reported later that President Roosevelt said that the loveliest sight he had seen on his entire trip was the Ward-Belmont campus with the white-clad girls lined along the drive.

The Demise of Ward-Belmont

From the perspective of 50 years later, it is initially very difficult to understand what happened to Ward-Belmont. Reading the news stories of 1951 raises many questions. Why would the board of a respected school turn its back on the school's excellent reputation and sell the extensive, well-equipped campus for a fraction of its value, especially when alumnae and friends were willing and able to raise an equivalent amount of money? Who stood to benefit from the transaction? What did the board believe would happen to the school after the sale of the property?

From the time of its founding until 1948, Ward-Belmont, like its predecessor institutions, was owned by stockholders. This form of ownership was not uncommon early in the twentieth century, when educators frequently established schools that they intended to run as profitable enterprises, much like any other business. During the Depression years, enrollment at Ward-Belmont declined, as it did at virtually all private schools; in the 1940s, there were approximately 600 students, down from a peak of more than 1,200 in the 1920s. Bank debts were incurred because income from tuition did not cover expenses. As a privately-owned institution, the school could not solicit aid from any educational foundation or establish an endowment fund to which alumnae could contribute.

FOND MEMORIES

Asked for memories of Ward-Belmont, Jeanne Gibson Bond (W-B '37) says, "There was such a feeling of 'belonging'—from the classes to the clubs, to the gym, to the extra-curricular activities, to the wonderful individual friendships—such a close camaraderie. It was truly one of the most meaningful experiences of my 81 years." Susan Winters Edwards (W-B '51) adds, "Attending an all-female school allowed us to hold offices, to plan and execute events, to participate in sports and to develop as much in an all-male world as we could. In those days, I believe a coed school would have meant mostly male class officers, etc., thus not permitting our responsible natures to grow."

Senior-Senior Middle Banquet 1937

WARTIME EFFORT

Although life of Ward-Belmont students centered on the campus, they were by no means isolated from the world at large, especially during the two world wars. The 1918 *Milestones* reported, "It would be strange if the fighting in France and the raising of a great army in America made no difference in our school life. Many of the girls spent part of their vacation making surgical dressings or helping in Red Cross membership drives and they were ready to respond to every appeal for service. Just before Christmas everybody began knitting. A few absent-minded girls ventured to class-rooms with knitting needles but no note-book. The lack of encouragement in this course may have caused its sudden abandonment. Even without the time lost to knitting by this insistence on the ordinary duties of the class-room, four hundred sweaters were sent."

Miss Morrison devised and planned a celebration to honor Colonel Luke Lea and the Tennesse troops he commanded when the World War I armistice was signed. Ward-Belmont girls formed a crepe paper replica of the American flag at the state Capitol.

When war was declared after the Japanese attack on Pearl Harbor on December 7, 1941, Dr. Provine called all the students to the auditorium to hear Mr. Roosevelt's speech on the radio. Some of the art students went to Union Station to sketch soldiers who were coming in and out. During the war some girls formed a group called TOPS (Training Offered for Patriotic Service). "We met for drill before breakfast three times a week and collected tinfoil, paper, cellophane and did other patriotic tasks. I remember being in a softball game in Club Village when we heard that Roosevelt had died and the TOPS put on a memorial parade in his honor," recalls Dr. Leotus "Leo" Morrison (W-B '46).

In 1948 Ward-Belmont was changed to a not-for-profit institution; in fact, there had been no profit for a number of years. This change was made for tax reasons and to meet the requirements of the Southern Association of Colleges and Secondary Schools. At that time the stockholders accepted bonds in payment for their stock, and the same board of directors that had represented the proprietary interests agreed to continue to serve until "a more suitable board" could be appointed. The members of this board were Dr. Robert Provine, president of Ward-Belmont; Brownlee O. Currey, president of Equitable Securities Corporation; L. M. Townsend, an officer of the Bank of New York and Trust Company; Warner McNeilly, president of the Nashville Trust Company; J. W. Miller, vice president of the First American National Bank; and Laurence B. Howard, a Nashville attorney.

By late 1950, the bond holders and the bank began to press for immediate payment of the debt. In addition, the Southern Education Association stipulated that every school under its jurisdiction must have an endowment sufficient to earn income of $17,500. Based on yields of about two percent on government bonds at the time, this would have required an endowment of $875,000.

Perhaps skeptical about the school's ability to establish such an endowment, or perhaps unwilling to make the necessary effort to raise a large sum of money, the board began to seek financial help from an institution willing and able to assume the school's indebtedness. They did not inform the alumnae or faculty of the school's financial situation, and no attempt was made to raise funds from alumnae or others.

In fact, the administration demonstrated little interest in maintaining contact with alumnae. In 1950, Mary Ann Moore, the new alumnae secretary on the Ward-Belmont staff, attended a seminar for people in similar positions at other private schools. When she returned, a member of the administration asked if the meeting had been worthwhile. Her answer was that it was very worthwhile and that she had heard again that it was very important to keep an up-to-date file of alumnae and to institute a program of alumnae giving. The administrator's comment was that giving did not apply in Ward-Belmont's situation. It is possible that negotiations were already in progress to change the school's ownership.

Apparently fearful that the school's reputation would be jeopardized if the potential accreditation problem were made public, the board quietly approached Vanderbilt, Peabody and several church organizations about taking over the school. Their efforts were unsuccessful until they contacted the Tennessee Baptist Convention.

George Washington Birthday Celebration

At the time the Tennessee Baptist Convention was preparing to spend about $750,000 to erect an office building in Nashville to serve as state headquarters. When this group learned that the Ward-Belmont property was available, they recognized an attractive opportunity. On February 15, 1951, Ward-Belmont's board of directors transferred ownership of the school to the Tennessee Baptist Convention. The Convention

THE FIRST WARD-BELMONT REUNION—1968

If there is any doubt that Ward-Belmont held a unique place in the hearts of its alumnae, that doubt would be dispelled by the wildly successful reunion held in 1968, 17 years after the school closed. Inspired by enjoyable gatherings that several Ward-Belmont classes had held, a few alumnae began to discuss the possibility of an all-school Ward-Belmont reunion in early 1968. The organizing committee—Sarah Bryan Benedict, Mary Elizabeth Cayce, Virginia Brown Moughon, Sarah Ophelia Colley Cannon (Minnie Pearl), Patty Chadwell, Jane Chadwell Delony and Virginia Smith Keathley, plus Rose Toney Hill as out-of-town chairman—thought that they might be able to gather at most 200 to 300 alumnae, and they decided it would be worth the effort.

Since alumnae lists were not relinquished when the school was sold, and there was no money for publicity, initial information about the event was mainly by word of mouth, transmitted by letter or telephone from friend to friend. After Virginia Keathley arranged for news of the reunion to be disseminated by the Associated Press, an astonishing number of responses began to come in from all over the country. Almost 900 alumnae from 37 states gathered in Nashville in March 1968 to reminisce, dance around the Maypole and participate in a gym class led by Miss Morrison. The president of Belmont College invited the alumnae for tea on the familiar old campus, and many Ward-Belmont alumnae first saw Harpeth Hall when Sarah Cannon (Minnie Pearl) hosted a fried chicken lunch there. The gathering became so large that the final banquet had to be moved from Belle Meade Club to the National Guard Armory.

Describing the reunion in her book *Gilly Goes to Ward-Belmont,* Gilbertine Moore (W-B '35) wrote, "Ward-Belmont was more than a place—it was a feeling, an experience, an emotion, an ideal, a tradition. It is for these reasons that it lives today in the hearts of thousands of alumnae around the world." Today, Miss Moore notes that Ward-Belmont was one of the five most influential experiences in her life. Those feelings led her to write her charming book, which provides a glimpse into the life of a young woman in the 1940s at Ward-Belmont.

assumed the debt, which totaled approximately $600,000. The value of the real estate, buildings, furnishings and equipment was estimated at $4 to $5 million.

The former Ward-Belmont board of trustees apparently believed that the new trustees would continue Ward-Belmont with "only such modifications as would make it conform to the Baptist system of education." Later it was revealed that these modifications called for the transfer of the College of Arts and Sciences of Cumberland University in Lebanon, Tennessee, to the Ward-Belmont campus. The college would therefore become coeducational, and it was unclear whether the preparatory school would continue at all. In addition, the Baptist group made plans to move their state offices to the campus. It soon became apparent that the group had the right to rent the school property for income purposes, even to the point of discontinuing the school if they so wished.

Nashville ~~Banner.~~

Nashville's Oldest Newspaper

LONG MAY OUR LAND BE BRIGHT WITH FREEDOM'S HOLY LIGHT; PROTECT US BY THY MIGHT, GREAT GOD, OUR KING

Weather Report
(By United States Weather Bureau)
NASHVILLE AND VICINITY—Cloudy with thundershowers tonight, low near 55; Thursday, showers and becoming colder.
TENNESSEE—Showers and thunderstorms tonight, low in the 40's northeast and in 50's west and south; Thursday, mostly cloudy, windy and turning colder.

Founded April 10, 1876

VOL. LXXV, NO. 277   NASHVILLE, TENN., WEDNESDAY AFTERNOON, FEB. 28, 1951   28 PAGES   PRICE: FIVE CENTS

$195 MILLION BUDGET REQUESTED

Baptists Take Over Ward-Belmont

The Drive to Save Ward-Belmont

Faculty, students, alumnae and friends learned of these developments from reports in the Nashville newspapers on February 28 and subsequent dates. The initial reaction was shock and disbelief. Soon alumnae and others who cared deeply about the loss of the school began to say, "Let's see what we can do about it."

On March 9, a group of alumnae and Nashville business people began working on two fronts: to raise money sufficient to regain control of the school and to negotiate with the Tennessee Baptist Convention.

Letters and pledge cards were sent out to alumnae and friends, local merchants were solicited, and Catherine Morrison, Ward-Belmont's popular athletic director, was sent to Texas to personally solicit contributions from the many wealthy alumnae there. The goal was $1 million, a sum that was believed to be adequate to persuade the Baptists to sell the property back to those who wanted to maintain Ward-Belmont. Alumnae and local business people responded quickly and positively. One alumna from Texas wrote, "We could have raised more than that just from Texas, if we had only known."

It was quickly determined that no legal means were available to reverse the transaction; the hope was that the buyers' group could be persuaded to see the situation from the point of view of those who loved the school and considered it important to the community.

Shortly after the announcement of the school's transfer to the Tennessee Baptist Convention, the alumnae secretary and a representative of the Nashville Ward-Belmont Alumnae Association met with Dr. Charles W. Pope, executive secretary of the Tennessee Baptist Convention, to express the wish of the alumnae to retain Ward-Belmont as a girls' school with its traditions and academic standing. Several further attempts were made to negotiate with Dr. Pope and with members of his executive board.

A group of Nashville alumnae began a highly organized letter-writing campaign to contact all the members of the Tennessee Baptist Convention to urge them to return Ward-Belmont to those who wanted to save the school. Alumnae and friends throughout the state contacted the individuals they knew personally, in the hope of exerting the greatest possible influence.

The Convention unfortunately refused to consider returning the property they had acquired at such a bargain. Their only commitment was to continue the school as it was for the remaining months of the 1951 school year. By late March, it was clear that Ward-Belmont would cease to exist. "Being in the last graduating class for the high school was a very touching and emotional time for all of us," says Susan Thomas Castner (W-B '51). "The last days at Ward-Belmont were so traumatic," recalls a faculty member. "All the teachers and students suffered through that last beautiful spring." Another teacher recalled Mrs. Souby at the last May Day celebration with tears streaming down her cheeks.

Graduation 1940

1950s

THE BEGINNINGS

As hope of saving Ward-Belmont faded, Nashville leaders concerned about education for girls began to take action. Motivated by a sense of urgency to continue quality education for girls in the community, a small and very dedicated group of volunteers worked with amazing speed to found a new school.

Dr. Daugh W. Smith and Mr. and Mrs. Foskett Brown together decided to call a meeting of people interested in preserving the academic standards and traditions of Ward-Belmont. The first organizational meeting was held on March 17, 1951, ironically in Acklen Hall of the school that had recently been lost.

In the course of the organizational meetings, attorney William Waller emerged as a key figure. Explaining how he became the first board chair, Mr. Waller modestly cited the need of the founding group for legal services "to obtain a corporate charter, look after the legal details of property acquisition, zoning matters, and so on."

Horace G. Hill, Jr., a long-time supporter of George Peabody College for Teachers, and Edith Caldwell Hill, a cousin of Miss Annie C. Allison, beloved principal of the high school department of Ward-Belmont, showed keen interest from the start. Besides their philosophical support of education for girls, the George Bullards and the Fred Russells had the more immediate need of education for their daughters.

Dr. Daugh W. Smith

Getting Organized

At a meeting on Easter Sunday, the founding group concluded that they could establish a new school provided Mrs. Susan Souby, the head of the high school department at Ward-Belmont, would agree to serve as head. When it became known that Peabody had offered Mrs. Souby an excellent position, a delegation promptly called on her. She confirmed that she was considering the offer from Peabody and expressed interest in the concept of creating a new school. As she evaluated her options, she was keenly aware of the substantial challenge involved in heading a new school, especially at age 60, when many people are considering retirement. One of her first steps was to undergo a complete physical examination. Assured that her health was good, she agreed to head the new school.

Finding a location for the new school became an immediate necessity. After considering several pieces of real estate, the group decided to purchase the P. M. Estes estate at the intersection of Hobbs Road and Estes Avenue. The central location of this impressive home and its spacious grounds were the deciding factors. The price for the 26 acres and the residence was $75,582. A commitment was made to purchase the property in early May, and the estate was officially acquired on July 1, 1951.

Individuals volunteered to chair the committees on which their interests and skills would be of greatest value. Active fund raising was launched immediately, led by George Bullard and Helen Bransford. The building committee appointed Hank Ingram as chairman to make improvements, additions and alterations to the property, with William Waller, Kermit Stengel and Mary Elizabeth Cayce (W-B '26) as assistants. The estimated cost to remodel the existing house turned out to be much greater than anticipated. The building committee therefore decided to leave the house as it was except for the addition of fire escapes and enclosing the southwest porch to provide a lunch room. Rather than providing for additional classrooms in the original house, plans were drawn for Little Harpeth, a new building with six classrooms, which could provide more space at a lower cost.

The architectural firm selected was Tisdale and Tisdale; financing of $125,000 was obtained through the National Life and Accident Insurance Company. Ground was broken for the new building by the end of July, with completion planned for soon after the opening of school. Little Harpeth was designed as a wing of the proposed auditorium/gymnasium building, but further construction would have to wait until additional funds could be raised. By the end of July, work had begun on the athletic field, tennis courts and the back driveway with the exit on Esteswood Avenue.

I was asked to take the post by some very lovely and charming ladies—among them: Dud Brown, Hortense Ingram, Ellen Hofstead, Mary Elizabeth Cayce, Edith Caldwell, Kay Russell and Helen Bransford. Some men might be able to turn such ladies down, but not I. My powers of resistance were totally inadequate. —William Waller

One task at hand was the selection of a name for the new school. An early settler in Middle Tennessee had given the name of Harpeth to the sloping hills and little river valley to the south of the campus. Focusing on this geographical position, Miss Cayce suggested the name of Harpeth Hall.

Enthusiastic Response

Mrs. Souby asked selected members of her Ward-Belmont faculty to give thought to continuing their teaching careers by joining her at Harpeth Hall. Assured that the new institution would be a college preparatory school in the tradition to which they were accustomed, and with tremendous confidence in Mrs. Souby, the faculty members responded positively. Patty Chadwell, a Ward-Belmont alumna and one of the original faculty members, said, "We were not told what we would be making. There were no contracts. It was all by word of mouth—no firm commitments at first. But I never had any doubts about the success of the new school. I never thought of *not* going, once they asked me."

On July 25, a letter went out to friends and parents of prospective students. Describing the school, it stated, "The purpose of Harpeth Hall is to help each student find in school the challenge of high intellectual aims, which will inspire her own best development. Special emphasis will be laid on thoroughness and serious interest in studies, on self control and consideration for others, and on the exercise of individual responsibility in all school activities." Parents were invited to return the application form with a deposit of $25 toward the first year's tuition of $400.

The response from parents of potential students was enthusiastic. The original plan had been to hold enrollment to 150 students for the first year. In order to accept all former Ward-Belmont students who wanted to continue their education in a similar environment, enrollment was increased to 161. "There was a lot of uncertainty, but relief, when we found we would have a school that was to be on the Estes estate and would have the same headmistress—Susan S. Souby—and many of the same teachers," noted Nancy Anne Holt Garver ('52).

Members of the community gave furniture and books, and faculty members donated their own books. Chairs were purchased from a restaurant that was going out of business. Miscellaneous items of all sorts turned up on the campus, and some use was found for anything that was offered. Miss Morrison gave each day student who was transferring to Harpeth Hall a hockey stick and a few costumes. Other items from Ward-Belmont mysteriously appeared on the campus.

HARPETH HALL'S ORIGINAL FACULTY

Margaret Ottarson
Latin

Lucie Fountain
French

Ella Puryear Mims
Spanish/Latin

Lenora Litkenhous
Art

Madeline Terry
Music

Catharine Winnia
Speech

Billie Kuykendall
English

Mary Rasmussen
English

Martha Gregory
English/Librarian

Frances Ewing
Mathematics

Ruth Mann
Mathematics

Penelope Mountfort
Science

Vera Brooks
History

Sophronia Eggleston
History

Patty Chadwell
Physical Education

Lucile McLean
Business Manager

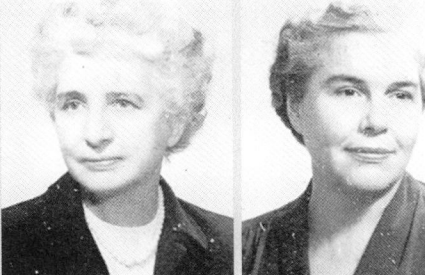
Vera Binkley
Dietitian

Roberta Wikle
Study Hall

C E L E B R A T I N G  M I L E S T O N E S

The Beginnings

"Mrs. Mann never sat still in algebra class. One day after no one could give the answer to whether the number in question should be 'plus or minus,' she ran around the room putting the correct answer on every chalk board, then jumped in the trash can. 'You girls upset me so, I'm just going to throw myself away!'" —Chloe Fort Lenderman ('58)

"Miss Penny impacted my life at this wonderful age, and I found Science through her humor and zest for living. She had gorgeous long, red hair and I admired her greatly—and went on to Vanderbilt University School of Nursing and practiced my profession for 30 years." —Sandy Travis Collier ('52)

"When I returned to school after my father died, two guardian angels beckoned gently to me. Penny Mountfort and Pat Moran carried me through many a bleak day that year and the next. To both of these wonderful, kind women and mentors, my eternal gratitude." —Kathy Starr Kaiser ('58)

A late July letter from Mr. Waller and Mrs. Souby concludes with a major understatement: "The successful launching of the school in so short a period of time is due to the fine cooperation of all concerned." It is almost unbelievable that in just four months a board and faculty were formed, funds to begin operation were secured, property was acquired, remodeling and new construction had begun, and 161 girls had enrolled. The amazing dedication, energy and cooperation of Harpeth Hall's founders serve as an inspiration to all who have benefited from their efforts. The title of Louise Douglas Morrison's (W-B '36) book about the founding of Harpeth Hall—*A Voyage of Faith*—is truly appropriate.

Harpeth Hall Opens Its Doors

September 17, 1951, was the first day at Harpeth Hall. "We were all huddled together until November," is the way Business Manager Lucile McLean described Harpeth Hall's space situation in its opening months. When 161 students, 15 faculty and three administrative staff members gathered for the first time at their new school, only two buildings were available for all classes and activities: the white brick home, now Souby Hall, and the small utility building which became the Senior House.

Perhaps it was because the campus lay in the heart of a residential neighborhood and had been designed with the grace of a family's home, rather than on a convenient busy thoroughfare, in a building with antiseptic linoleum floors and walls of concrete block, that the students so quickly learned to treat it with respect and pride. Souby Hall, with its black and white marble foyer, spiral staircase, chandeliers and red carpet, and the

several tile and marble bathrooms off the upstairs bedrooms/classrooms tended to project the feeling of homey embrace as the students took their seats for their classes. The privacy of the campus and intimacy of the small classrooms with their large windows filled with sunlight produced a sheltering effect for the student.

Creative Classrooms

A bit of resourcefulness and creativity were required in utilizing a house as a new school. Ruth Mann's math classes sat around the kitchen work table with pots and pans still hanging from a rack overhead. The science class was located next to the main office near the south porch windows in order to get enough light for the microscopes to work. Fireplaces were abundant, welcoming Mary Rasmussen's English students upstairs and Margaret (Pat) Ottarson's Latin students in the sunporch downstairs. A third fireplace was in the front parlor which became the first library and study hall (now the Ward-Belmont Room). Kay Baker Gaston ('58)

remembers, "The library was the most welcoming room in the school. Mrs. Rasmussen's reading list was choice, the world's best books. I think I have finally read them all. What a discriminating reader she was!"

A few desks set up in the basement (which Roberta "Ro" Wikle named the Mole Run) became a small make-do study hall. Even after there was study space elsewhere, the ping-pong table and the first lockers remained in these two rooms at the bottom of the basement stairs.

On opening day Harpeth Hall had no cafeteria, no uniforms and no gymnasium or athletic field. A large bell hung between Souby Hall and the Senior House and was rung by Miss Wikle to indicate period changes. It was given to the school by Mrs. John Early, mother of board member Mrs. Fred Russell and grandmother of students Kay Russell Beasley ('52), Ellen Russell Sadler ('55), Carolyn Russell ('64) and Lee Russell Brown ('60).

Students stayed only half the day and brought food from home for the one short break in an accelerated schedule. Sandy Travis Collier ('52) describes the attire: "We wore dirty saddle oxfords (never polished) and white ankle socks with lace on them. We wore our fathers' white button-down collar dress shirts tied in a knot in the front."

Patty Chadwell, "Miss Patty," did not let lack of equipment or a building deter her from insisting on physical education for everyone. During the summer, she had spent a lot of time looking for two trees the right distance apart to tie up a volleyball net. A local sporting goods company let her search their attic for outdated balls and nets. In addition to volleyball and ping pong, Miss Patty had her students practice carrying a hockey stick correctly while jogging up and down the hill. Classes marched in formation. At the command, "Dress right," a straight line was to be formed and attendance recorded. Students called out their number or were marked absent. Miss Patty also recruited Patsy Neblett Moran (W-B '41) as a volunteer assistant who remained enthusiastic enough to join the faculty after finishing college to teach and coach until 1996.

Bullard Gym 1954

"Dress Right"

PATTY CHADWELL

For Patty Litton Chadwell, the fountain of youth has surely been her association with Harpeth Hall. For half a century "Miss Patty"—as she is widely and lovingly known—has been involved with the school, from its founding to the present. This distinction is hers alone and one of which she is very proud.

Born in Nashville on June 9, 1915, "Miss Patty" grew up on a farm off Gallatin Road where she lived in her great-grandfather Isaac Litton's home along with her parents and sister. It was there that she began her lifelong love of tennis when she and her cousins built a tennis court in a pasture.

Miss Patty graduated from Ward-Belmont Junior College in 1935 and later received a Masters Degree in Physical Education at Peabody College (now a part of Vanderbilt University). Her love of Ward-Belmont drew her back to her alma mater where she taught physical education for six years before joining Harpeth Hall with Mrs. Souby in 1951.

After 30 years as head of the physical education department and teacher of a variety of sports, she retired in 1981. However, hardly a week goes by that she is not at Harpeth Hall for some reason. The physical education department that Miss Patty began half a century ago has grown exponentially. She now marvels at the growth from the time when tennis was the only team sport offered at Harpeth Hall to the present, when two gyms are hardly enough space to offer physical education classes and team sports.

Of all the changes that Miss Patty has seen in the 50 years of growth and development at Harpeth Hall, one element remains constant: the overwhelming gratification that she has received by teaching and being involved with the "girls." In a fitting tribute to her, there is now a statewide tennis tournament for high school teams, the Patty Chadwell Invitational, and the upper tennis courts are named in her honor. She has represented dignity and grace to generations of "girls," and it is this that has carried her through her active life.

At Commencement on May 29, 2000, Miss Patty was honored with the Dede Bullard Wallace Award. This award is occasionally given to honor persons who have made an outstanding contribution to the school. After the thrill and surprise of receiving this award, Miss Patty was asked, "How did you happen to be there (at Commencement)?" Her reply was, "I didn't *happen* to be there, I am *always* there."

Student Life

Little Harpeth, the new academic building, was completed in November, providing a science lab and classrooms for languages, math, history and art. English classes remained upstairs in Souby Hall and there was now space for offices downstairs, a faculty room, a kitchen for food preparation and a combination study hall/lunchroom/auditorium for the regular weekly school assemblies. It was two rooms actually, so that speakers were forced to stand in a doorway between the two and look first one way and then the other to make eye contact with the audience.

Although the faculty enjoyed the lunches during those early years, Miss Patty remembers that the students "wouldn't touch the food." Language teacher Ella Puryear Mims recalls spinach with hardboiled eggs and other delicious dishes. Students, however, quickly dismissed the plate lunches with mushrooms and almonds, pimento cheese or carrot sandwiches.

With expanded space, the school schedule settled into a more normal routine—academic classes until three o'clock with a break for lunch and club sports afterwards. Every student carried a four-course academic load and regular gym classes at least three times a week.

THE ORIGIN OF THE FOUR CLUBS

The students at Ward-Belmont were originally divided into two groups, the Panthers and the Regulars, for sports competition. By 1922, there were enough girls that two more groups were added, the Olympians and the Athenians. Each of these groups included day and boarding students, high school and college.

In the meantime, 10 social clubs had been established for boarders. These clubs, which hosted dances, day trips and other events, were the center of social life for boarding students. When these clubs began competing in athletics, two groups were formed for day students: the Di Gammas and the Betas. This arrangement did not work very well because the day students always won everything. Many of the day students attended Ward-Belmont for six years, while most of the boarders were there for just two years. Many of the boarders had come from small towns, where they had had little opportunity to swim or play tennis, and most had never heard of hockey. The boarders suggested that the day students should be divided into four groups to even the competition.

By 1927, it was decided to establish four clubs for the day students. A girl was chosen from the second year college class to organize and lead each group. Each of these leaders chose five girls to form the nucleus of her group: a freshman, sophomore, junior, junior middle (fourth year high school), and senior middle (first year college). Four colors were chosen, and each group drew a number and by its number chose red, blue, yellow or green. Then each group selected a teacher as sponsor.

With Mary Elizabeth Cayce (W-B '26) as their leader, the blue group chose the name of the ancient Cambodian city Angkor Wat. This beautiful city was considered the eighth wonder of the world, and the Angkors intended to be another wonder. Emma Elizabeth Green Bogle (W-B '26) and her yellow group chose the name Ariston, a name they derived from the Greek word *aristokratia*, which means "rule by the best." The third color drawn was red, so the red group called themselves the Triads, drawing on the Latin word for "three." Their leader was Dibbie Barthell Vaughn (W-B '28), who later moved to New York and became a blues singer on the radio. The green group selected the Native American name Eccowasin, which meant "be all and give all." Their leader was Mary Brandon Spivey (W-B '28) from Springfield, Tennessee.

The next step was a week-long period of rush to choose members for each club; the process was essentially the same as that used by the boarding students' clubs. At the end of the week, each group turned in a preferential list and each girl put down her choices in order. Then a matching process took place. No girl was left out, and no one knew whether she had been on a preferential list or not.

In the fall of 1945, college day students were incorporated into the 10 clubs that had previously been all boarders. This left the Angkors, Aristons, Triads and Eccowasins as groups of high school day students. When these four clubs were transferred to Harpeth Hall, it was decided that drawing names for members would replace rushing. Any girl whose sister, mother or grandmother had been in a club could request to be in the same one.

Some students chose to add art classes or glee club, and everyone held membership in one of the four school clubs: Angkor, Ariston, Eccowasin or Triad. Outside the classroom, the four school clubs generated most of the action. Everyone belonged; everyone could participate in her own way. The clubs organized service projects, competed for the best grades, the most citizenship points and for the yearly athletic championship. Rivalry was enthusiastic with cheerleaders and many spectators at the after-school games. Varsity players were selected from the best among all the club teams. The girl named the outstanding athlete had participated in the most sports and won more points either individually or by her team's performance.

There were special interest clubs in languages, science, art and music as well as Penstaff for creative writing. Some extras were not optional. Freshmen came one morning a week before classes began for word study and then for Bible (as literature) taught by Mrs. Souby. Sophomores had training in speech; juniors studied hygiene; and seniors learned first aid. By 1960 general science and economic geography had been added to the course offerings.

Students elected seniors to the student council as their governing body. The first *Milestones* yearbook wrote that "they uphold the standards of the school." A specific duty was to assign penalties for infractions of school rules. Other leadership positions existed in classes, clubs and athletics, and this opportunity appealed to both past and potential Harpeth Hall students.

> *Harpeth Hall was the best education I ever had, and I teach in college now. But more than the preparation, Harpeth Hall gave me the dignity of being a woman that was hard to find back then, either at home or in the world, and that sense of self carried me through and still carries me. —Sharon Mayhall Rush ('60)*

The First Leader

"Her door was always open to faculty members and students," is the way that Miss Mims described Susan S. Souby's school presence. She placed her office in a central location just off the large front hall near the main door, in the wood-paneled library quite appropriate for a school's leader. Her judgment was sound; the room remains the office of the head of school today. Lucile McLean, business manager, initially shared the room with Mrs. Souby, and, using her typewriter and the only telephone, did all the necessary buying, selling, collecting and disbursing so that Mrs. Souby could spend her time with students and faculty.

Mrs. Souby preferred the title of director to either principal or headmistress, and the title well describes the way she translated her clear vision of young women's education into reality. Founding parents and board members were convinced that the proven Ward-Belmont educational experience could continue in this new setting and that Mrs. Souby would provide the leadership to make success possible.

With a faculty in place, all but one of whom stayed throughout Harpeth Hall's crucial first decade, Mrs. Souby contacted the admissions officers of the many colleges and universities to which she had sent students in the past to inform them of her new situation. They all assured her that as long as she remained as the head of the school, her graduates would receive the same consideration as they had always.

The matter of accreditation was a bit more complicated. Knowing that one of the requirements of the Southern Association of Colleges and Schools was a trained librarian, Mrs. Souby asked Martha Gregory to attend the School of Library Science at George Peabody College for Teachers to qualify for the position, even though she also was teaching freshman English. She acted as librarian for only a few years before returning to the classroom full-time. When she retired from teaching in 1983, she remained at Harpeth Hall, assisting Librarian Mary Lee Matthews Manier (W-B '42) on a part-time basis in the much larger Annie C. Allison Library.

Other requirements involved submitting written reports to the Association about every aspect of the school's operation. The culminating event was a campus visit by the accrediting committee who, for three days, interviewed faculty and students, sat in on classes and generally watched the school in action. All the results were favorable and Harpeth Hall gained official accreditation in its very first year of operation.

SUSAN S. SOUBY

In a newspaper profile written in the midst of her tenure as headmistress, Mrs. Susan Souby described Harpeth Hall as "a world of young women and I'll admit they're my living and my being." Of her job, Mrs. Souby went on to say: "I like the girls and that's the important thing about my job. I've spent so many years with them and watched them grow into young women that they have become my only life."

Those who knew Mrs. Souby say her quotes accurately capture what Harpeth Hall meant to her and what she meant to the school. "She was a wonderful educator," remembers Frances H. Ewing, one of the 15 teachers who were at Harpeth Hall when it began. "Her first priority was that the teachers knew their subjects and her second was to know each teacher and each student personally. She was not just the headmistress, she was our friend."

Mrs. Souby began her career as an English teacher at Ward-Belmont in 1924 shortly after the death of her husband, A.M. Souby. When Annie Allison retired as principal in 1945, Mrs. Souby took over. Following the demise of Ward-Belmont in the spring of 1951, Mrs. Souby agreed to become headmistress of Harpeth Hall, which was chartered and operating by fall of the same year.

"With the changeover from Ward-Belmont, steeped in its tradition, to Harpeth Hall, many Nashvillians wondered if the new school would last," Mrs. Souby told the newspaper reporter in 1957. "Most people didn't express their doubts to me until the school was established, then I realized they had some misgivings." Some of those misgivings were probably eased by the fact that the new school became accredited a little more than a year after its opening, which, at the time, was a record for a private preparatory school. Mrs. Souby credited the faculty for its help. "I was fortunate to get 12 of my teachers from Ward-Belmont to come with me."

Getting the school going took all of her time, Mrs. Souby admitted. "I have very little time outside the school," she said in the article. She did admit to two hobbies: collecting recipes she never had time to use and gardening, which she satisfied by walking Harpeth Hall's campus.

The one thing Mrs. Souby had time for was the students. She set the schedules for all students and spent a lot of time in her office and in study hall, working one-on-one with students. Here's how the newspaper article described her relationship with her students: "Not only does Mrs. Souby help her girls with their studies, but she is often called upon to help them with their personal problems. Seldom does she leave the campus before late in the evening and many are the Saturdays and Sundays she has spent there attending to details that had to be left undone because her time had been consumed with one girl's problem. Her alert analysis of children has helped her to begin personally knowing each girl from the first day of fall classes."

Mrs. Souby, who had two sons, Max and Edward, and generations of students at Ward-Belmont and Harpeth Hall, retired in 1963 and died the following year in 1964.

In her retirement speech, language teacher Ella Puryear Mims put Mrs. Souby's relationship to her faculty a little more simply: "You have given us the ideals by which we have taught." Miss Mims also said in her speech that she would not be a "true student" of Mrs. Souby's if she didn't end her tribute with a few lines of English poetry. These lines, she said, perfectly captured Mrs. Souby:

The reason firm, the temperate will, / Endurance, foresight, strength and skill,

A perfect woman, nobly planned, / To warn, to comfort and command;

And yet a spirit still, and bright / With something of angelic light.

The First Graduation

"I have the pleasure of addressing my first graduating class and my first group of alumnae at the same time," remarked Mrs. Souby on June 4, 1952. She spoke proudly to the graduates and the assembled guests, stating, "We shall pay our debt to the past by putting the future in debt to us" and reminding them that at "this time last year we did not even have a school." The class of 1952 managed in their one Harpeth Hall year to publish a yearbook, put on Shakespeare's *As You Like It* on the same outdoor stage from which they would receive their diplomas and raise money for a class gift—the piano which would accompany the graduation ceremony. "I always considered myself a Harpeth Hall graduate," says Mary Schlater Stumb ('53). She completed two years at Ward-Belmont but gives credit to the new school for "a terrific education, the desire to always keep learning, happy times then and now, and skills to help cope with difficult times." This sentiment is echoed by members of all three of the transferring upper classes. They knew the rules; they knew what to expect in classes; they were the solid base on which to build the future.

I still remember our white dresses, red roses, walking across the stage and the wonderment of being the first graduation class. —Dixie Glover Heagy ('52)

Many graduates chose to study at Vanderbilt University. About one-third started there, and others transferred after two years away from Nashville. Other acceptances included Harvard/Radcliffe, Sweet Briar, Northwestern, Lindenwood College, Southern Methodist University, College of Wooster, Southwestern at Memphis (Rhodes College), Columbia University, Stephens College, Universities of Kentucky and Tennessee, Mary Baldwin and Agnes Scott.

Additions to the school would continue in the following years—bigger buildings, new courses and teachers, more student activities and publications—but there was no doubt on that June evening that Harpeth Hall was firmly launched into the future.

New Symbols for Old Ways

Although classes and teachers continued much as they had been previously at Ward-Belmont, some traditions changed to fit their new setting. "The Bells of Ward-Belmont" were no longer present at the corner of Hobbs and Estes; Harpeth Hall needed its own song to sing. Mrs. Gregory occasionally brought a guitar into her freshman English classroom and sang with them, especially when ballads were being studied. She included these freshmen as she began to compose a new alma mater. Lissa Luton Bradford ('55) recalled a discussion about school colors. "We insisted on magnolia green and silver gray, not just any ordinary green and gray. Mrs. Gregory led us to make suggestions about the words, but most of the real work was hers."

ALMA MATER

O Harpeth Hall, O place beloved,
Thy beauty crowns the hills;
In strength and grace thy walls arise
Above the woodland still.
Our voices ring with happiness,
Our hearts are filled with pride,
As here each girl finds for herself
The joys that will abide.

So light of heart and free we pledge
Allegiance through the years,
As old girls with the new girls share
The pleasure that endears.
Thy standard from the hillside waves
In dark magnolia green
And of thy destiny so fair
Proud privilege to sing!

Joyce Crutcher Ward ('60), a Latin teacher since 1968, expanded on the magnolia image in a 1998 issue of the *Hallways* alumnae publication. She wrote that "the magnolia had for centuries in China symbolized the magnificence of womanhood, and in Victorian England and America, represented nobility of soul and purity of heart. In the dark days of the American Civil War, the flower came to stand for the strength, courage and beauty of southern women. For all these reasons, magnolia green is one of our school colors and why the Lady of the Hall and her court carry a single magnolia blossom at Step Singing."

Designing an emblem to represent Harpeth Hall was undertaken by Mrs. Souby and Pat Ottarson, who taught Latin and was accomplished in several other ancient languages as well—even Sanskrit. They envisioned a seal in the school colors, a graphic design to serve as letterhead for school stationery and embroidered on banners and, later, printed on mugs and other gift items. And there would be a motto, some words significant to the Harpeth Hall experience.

The finished design pictured a lamp of learning at the center in front of an open book encircled by the Latin phrase *Mentem spiritumque tollamus,* "Let us lift up the mind and the spirit." The burning flame of the ancient Greek lamp represents the wisdom of the past and illuminates the books that hold the ideas and knowledge, which continue to enhance both mind and spirit.

Lady of the Hall

Ward-Belmont's May Day was an elaborate festival at which all students performed dances to entertain the May Queen who arrived in a carriage drawn by a team of horses. Though Harpeth Hall had no horses, no carriage and no dance department in the early years, it was still appropriate to have a ceremony to honor the senior voted by the students to be most representative of the ideals of the school.

The title for this outstanding young woman would now be Lady of the Hall rather than May Queen. In the spring of 1952, the sophomores, all of whom studied speech, performed a play. The long porch on the south side of Souby Hall was a perfect stage. Students selected from younger classes to be heralds announced the Lady of the Hall as she and her attendants plus a young crown bearer walked across the porch and down the steps onto the lawn. They took their seats in front of a large screen decorated by the junior class to create a pretty background.

The background screen consisted of a chicken wire frame woven with Virginia creeper vine which grew on trees all over the campus. Mrs. Souby would put on her boots, gloves and hat and take her clippers to accompany the girls to be sure they knew the difference between Virginia creeper and poison ivy as they gathered the greenery. Later the screen was covered with green crepe paper and white napkins so it could be stored and used another year.

In 1977, the program was revamped and moved to Sunday. Combined with Step Singing, the event then took place on the north side of Souby Hall. In 1987, the ceremony was moved to the front of the library where graduation had been held since 1967.

Step Singing

Step Singing was a long-established year-end event at Ward-Belmont. Seniors lined the three steps that spanned the front of the academic building, hence the name Step Singing, to sing the traditional songs *a capella*. At Harpeth Hall, the steps in front of Souby Hall became the first stage, and the daisy chain laid down on the lawn in front of the singers to spell out the numbers of the class year was originally made by students from wild field daisies. Also at Step Singing, the junior class is officially recognized as the new senior class and joins in reciting the pledge to the school, familiar to graduates of both Ward-Belmont and Harpeth Hall.

THE PLEDGE

We will respect and obey the school's laws and will do our best to incite a like respect in those around us who are prone to annul them or set them at naught. We will strive unceasingly to quicken our mutual sense of duty. Thus, in all these ways, we will transmit this school not less, but greater, better and more beautiful than it was transmitted to us.

THE POPCORN INCIDENT

In 1955, a student brought an electric popcorn popper to the Senior House, looking forward to an easy between-meal snack, not realizing that cooking was forbidden without permission. Since it is almost impossible to hide the aroma of fresh corn popping, the machine was soon discovered, and Mrs. Souby acted to make sure that all the seniors understood the seriousness of the situation. "What do you think your citizenship grade should be?" She put this difficult question to each senior in a private conference. She reminded them of the school's honor system and then asked them to decide whether their knowledge of, or involvement with, the popcorn popper constituted good or poor citizenship. Whatever they told her became the grade that was recorded for them on the next report card. Class members still say it was one of the hardest answers they ever had to determine.

George and Martha Washington

The first mention of a George Washington's Birthday Celebration is in the 1920 *Milestones*, which described Washington's birthday as "a great day at Ward-Belmont." The glowing description continues: "The artistic grace with which Ward-Belmont girls assumed the roles of Colonial dames and gentlemen will remain unsurpassed. Who would have

guessed that some of the most beautiful ladies were wearing their window draperies for panniers, or that many of the beaux were dressed in gymnasium bloomers and uniform coat turned lining side out! Martha and George were charming as they came down the stairs, followed by a company of loyal attendants. There were Thomas Jeffersons, John Quincy Adams, Nathan Hales, Patrick Henrys, Paul Reveres and Lafayettes, not to mention lovely Betsy Rosses and sisters, wives and sweethearts of the patriots."

In 1954, Patty Chadwell renewed the celebration at Harpeth Hall with only freshmen participating. "It grew out of the things the students had learned," she said. Freshmen marched in gym class and did research in English class on persons of the same era that they most wanted to be. They voted on two members of the junior class to preside over the festivities as George and Martha. Some costumes had been salvaged from Ward-Belmont, but evening dresses with shawls and men's suit coats turned inside out, even pajama pants were transformed to fit the occasion. Today, the George Washington Celebration is performed by the seventh grade class as their American history studies coincide nicely with the pageant. They select members of the eighth grade class to play the roles of George and Martha.

Different Rules for Different Spaces

An elected student government and Honor Council remained in place to monitor behavior. While the old constraints against chewing gum and talking to boys on campus transferred from Ward-Belmont to Harpeth Hall, students began to put their own distinguishing marks on the new school.

The incoming freshmen, class of '55, perhaps because they never had attended Ward-Belmont, led the way in creating the need for new rules. First came the great wild onion eradication effort. Each class chose a school service project and this one was designed to beautify the old formal garden. The steps leading into the garden had been the setting for the official portrait of the Lady of the Hall and her court. The harsh ice storm in the winter of 1951 had ruined many trees and other plantings all over town so there was much work to be done on campus. Some progress was certainly made to eliminate the ubiquitous bulb, but another consequence was both unexpected and more spectacular. Someone found the turn-on spigot for the water! The multitiered fountain rose from the center of a small pool which had no water in it at the time and was so tall that to see into the top basin a person had to step across the pool, balance by holding onto the middle of the fountain and stretch upwards. Freshmen began to lure unsuspecting upperclassmen to see the huge spider in the top of the fountain and then turn on the water as they looked! It became against the rules to turn on the water the day that science teacher Miss Penny Mountfort was persuaded to step up and view the spider.

Freshmen also discovered the tangle of old grapevines in the trees behind Kirkman House before there was a Middle School or track down the hill toward the front gate. It was a perfect place to gather after lunch out of sight and free to talk and swing. Unfortunately, it took too long to return up the hill to class when the bell rang, or at least that was the reason given for the rule against going to the grapevines during school hours.

Bullard Gym—1954

"A very personable and capable man," was George N. Bullard, according to Dr. Daugh Smith, another person who was in on the making of Harpeth Hall from the beginning. Bullard served as the first treasurer of the board of trustees and became an effective fund-raiser. From the beginning, the school founders and first contributors knew that Harpeth Hall's physical plant would need more classrooms, a gym and an auditorium right away. Appeals to potential supporters began immediately. Sufficient funds were raised in the first months to build the classrooms and tennis courts and to construct a level, grassy athletic field and a back driveway into the school property off Esteswood Avenue, but not enough to build the gym. For two entire seasons, club basketball games had to be played on Saturday mornings at Robertson Academy, a public elementary school several miles south of Harpeth Hall. In case of rain, outdoor ceremonies such as graduation and Step Singing had no indoor place on campus to use, and any play or program to which a large number of guests might be invited was out of the question. A dedicated George Bullard led the effort to complete the plans already formulated for the gymnasium/auditorium building which would extend northward from Little Harpeth's classrooms. [*Editor's Note:* His daughter Dede Bullard Wallace was honored as Lady of the Hall in 1953. *See* page 58.]

Athletics and other activities expanded immediately into this fine new space on campus. Basketball and volleyball moved inside; students had lockers and showers; and Miss Patty occupied a real office. The number of varsity sports expanded from four to six, allowing for more club sport competitions.

The length of the playing surface extended beyond the basketball goal at one end to give room for chairs and a podium to be set up for the all-school assemblies. Various programs or reports by students or guests might be presented at these meetings, and Wednesdays were for chapel. Each week a different local minister was invited by the student council to speak. The hymn was always the same: "We Gather Together To Ask The Lord's Blessing."

Rhythmics was added to the gym classes. It was not dance or aerobics, but girls practiced walking with proper posture and sitting down in a ladylike fashion. Under Miss Patty's stern direction no slouching or crossed knees were allowed.

A SIGN OF THE TIMES

As the threat of a nuclear attack by the U.S.S.R. escalated in the 1950s, the U.S. government and private citizens took precautions. Under President Eisenhower's directive, roads were built and plans made to evacuate and hide government leaders. Many citizens constructed private bomb shelters with weeks of provisions to shut themselves away from the air and water contamination that would follow an explosion.

A group of senior chemistry students from Harpeth Hall, who were studying nuclear energy, visited the Oak Ridge Laboratories in Oak Ridge, Tennessee. There, they understood that Tennessee would be a prime attack target because of the atomic fuel production capabilities at Oak Ridge. A team of students, therefore, drew up a plan for warnings in case of a potential attack and for safe places on campus for everyone to go. The option of ordering a metal identification "dog tag" was available. Time was allotted for a practice run.

The most obvious effect at the time was increased awareness of world affairs. A lasting effect was the realization that the future was no longer as certain as had been expected.

Graduation Dance 1957

Tea Dance

The very first all-school prom, possible now because of the spacious gym, was a Tea Dance. Taking place for two hours in the late afternoon, it was still formal though dresses were just above the ankles "tea length," rather than to the floor "evening length." White gloves were essential. Students decorated the gym; punch and cookies were served, and all the faculty came to chaperone. Before any dancing began, every girl introduced her escort to each teacher as they sat in a long row around the room. The same polite ritual was expected to take place at most social gatherings the students attended.

Clear ideals of behavior existed at Harpeth Hall as well as in the '50s culture that surrounded it. Susan Moore ('53) remembers a teacher telling her that it was "presupposed that a young woman would be a lady," a word whose definition in the twenty-first century may well be perceived differently than it was then. At its best, being ladylike was not meant to be restrictive; rather it indicated that a person would act on any occasion in an appropriate way. Good manners, proper speech and respect for discipline and for those in authority effectively smoothed the paths of daily living for everyone. Parents and teachers sometimes used "Be a lady" to counteract what they considered excesses—too boisterous in manner, too much argument in speaking, too unorthodox in dress—because they valued the even flow of their lives and wanted to pass their achievements on to the next generation.

Citizenship Award

Harpeth Hall has always honored its outstanding citizens as well as its scholars. A letter grade was reported each grading period based on the positive values of leadership, cooperation and fair play that teachers and administrators saw students exhibit at school day to day. In the '50s, the senior with the most points was awarded the Citizenship Bracelet; today these respected awards are given to a girl in each class.

IN MEMORIAM

Dede Bullard was a member of the original student body of Harpeth Hall. She graduated in 1953 and was chosen Lady of the Hall that year. While at Harpeth Hall she helped establish the spirit of this new school by being involved in all phases of campus life. After graduating, she entered the Nashville community with the same spirit of involvement.

After her untimely death in October of 1969, the board of trustees established the Dede Bullard Wallace Award in her memory. The award is presented periodically for recognition of conspicuous achievement and contribution to Harpeth Hall. Since its first presentation in 1974 to Dr. Martha Overholser, there have been 14 recipients of this coveted award: Dr. Daugh W. Smith, Idanelle McMurry, Polly Fessey, Mary Elizabeth Cayce, Jeanne Zerfoss, Tracy Caulkins, Polly Jordan Nichols, Robert W. Kitchel, Britton and Norris Nielsen, Mary Schlater Stumb, Susan McKeand Baughman, Lindy Sayers, Jackie Glover Thompson and Patty Chadwell.

Ellen Kathleen Wray died from cancer on February 14, 1955, during her last high school semester. In three and one-half years at Harpeth Hall, she was an example of living life fully, even with an artificial leg and in failing health. As the 1955 *Milestones* tribute records, her friends knew her "soft smile floating into quiet laughter, sweeping away trivialities, a firm yet gentle hand, guiding some, following others and a calmness so deep that it steadied those about her." They also remembered her thoughtful intelligence and outstanding grades, which led classmates to urge that the commencement award for the highest academic average in the senior class be named the Katie Wray Award in her memory. This coveted award continues today.

Dede Bullard
(top step center)

Katie Wray
(third from left)

The Impact of a Harpeth Hall Education

Martha Grizzard Upshaw ('54), 1954 Lady of the Hall, sums up many graduates' feelings about attending Harpeth Hall: "Harpeth Hall opened up a whole new world to me. The idea that a small group of people could create a large new institution was unfamiliar and quite amazing. In that first year, I learned the real meaning of commitment. Mrs. Souby and her staff were pillars of strength, and the fact that they were women had a very special impact on me.

"The '50s were not a time of radical change for most women, but for me, a door was opened. I gained self-confidence I never would have had if I had not been at Harpeth Hall. Supported by the unparalleled education I received, I was not afraid to make some difficult choices when conflicts later arose with my parents and when major cultural issues shook the nation in the '60s and '70s. I am indeed grateful to Harpeth Hall for instilling in me a powerful love of learning. I am certain that it has made me a better marriage partner, a better parent and a better citizen."

By 1960 Harpeth Hall was firmly established in its own image. It continued to build on the strength of Ward-Belmont's past and pushed ahead to maintain a leading edge in educating young women. The world was about to undergo a series of major changes, and Harpeth Hall graduates would be ready.

Tea Dance 1958

Spanish Club

ENROLLMENT INCREASES

In 1955, this first freshman class, now seniors, was still the school's smallest at 28, but the number of freshmen had risen to over 60. As Harpeth Hall's reputation in the community grew, so did the number of students who applied each year. From 1956 on, the total enrollment was above 200, and the faculty was enlarged from 18 to 22. Today with the addition of grades fifth through eighth in the Middle School and much expanded facilities, the student population numbers 543 and the teaching faculty 73.

1970s

THE TIDES OF CHANGE

Changes in American life and society that started in the 1960s continued in the 1970s. Later, Americans would look back wistfully to the "simpler" times before these two decades brought with them alterations in laws, technology, schools, even neighborhoods that affected the way Americans lived their lives.

"Change" became as much a mantra for the 1970s as it had been for the 1960s. It seemed that no institution, from the government to the church to the family to small independent girls' schools, escaped vast changes. And yet the day-to-day workings and student life at Harpeth Hall were largely tranquil. Big changes were usually evident only as accretions of small changes. A class was added here, a building built there. Even as the ground shifted under them, seniors were still seniors, scared to graduate but ready to fly. Juniors were still juniors, longing for the respect and privileges conferred by seniorhood. Freshmen and sophomores were still as angst-ridden as ever. Girls still fretted over their figures, spent sunny days tanning behind the gym and wondered how they would ever get through *War and Peace*.

New Roles—and Regulations

Who would have thought that a tucked-away independent girls' school in a medium-size city would experience the convergence of two big societal shifts in the 1970s? But that's exactly what happened to Harpeth Hall as the women's movement encouraged a generation of young women to work full-time outside the home and court-enforced busing sent students to a bizarre patchwork of schools.

Middle School Eccowasin Club 1970

Working women, however, were just one aspect of that earthquake called the women's movement. From the straightforward book *Our Bodies Ourselves* to the National Organization for Women to the Equal Rights Amendment to *Roe v. Wade*, women were shaking off old roles and rules and experimenting with new ones.

This spirit of freedom from past restraints was reflected even in the small aspects of young women's lives. Fussy, coiffed hair fell out of fashion, and long hair was the trend. Candice Graf Ohl ('70) recalls that, "We all wore our hair long, with side curlicues; mine was parted on the side. . . (We used) Dippity-Do and big curlers."

Freer bodies meant that women's hemlines crept up and up, and the styles got bolder and bolder. "Until then we were all wearing Villager and Lady Bug and skirts and sweaters and Weejuns," remembers Cathy Ellis Connery ('72). "It was like a very clear demarcation that hit in about 1971 or '72. Suddenly everyone was wearing those Mexican blouses you could buy in Hillsboro Village. I had this electric blue pair of crushed velvet bell-bottoms with a macrame belt and a top that snapped at the crotch and was psychedelic. And I wore it to school! That probably was the outfit that sent them to uniforms."

From about the late 1960s forward, Harpeth Hall's board of trustees debated uniforms each year, with the "nays" a bare majority. The decision was delayed in 1971 when it was decreed that students could wear pants. The following year,

Headmistress Idanelle McMurry made the executive decision to adopt uniforms. These were optional for seniors and for the junior class. Even with uniforms, the skirt controversy raged on. "They were so short! I don't know how we sat down!" said one alumna. Finally it was decreed that the skirts would be no shorter than three inches above the knee. "It was my worst job," says then-Student Council President Beth Lewis Murphy ('71) of enforcing the hem law. "I used to beg my friends: 'Please, please don't make me send you home.'" Lewis had been given the job by the faculty, who also disliked the task.

Suitable subjects for study were changing, too. As the 1970s opened, the senior class president and a student council representative requested that the school add courses in philosophy and in the "soft sciences" of psychology and sociology. Harpeth Hall students who wanted to study physics went to courses at Montgomery Bell Academy, a nearby boys' school. Harpeth Hall started a chapter of the Cum Laude Society in 1973 to recognize academic excellence. Entrance in the society was the school's highest academic honor.

These moves solidified the school's reputation as challenging and demanding. The Winterim program was another academic and professional stride forward. The program was established in the 1972-1973 school year by Miss McMurry, who charged Peter Minton, the first dean of the Upper School, with executing the initial efforts. The goal of Winterim was to give girls an opportunity to learn a new skill or sport, work at an internship off-campus or travel abroad to experience a different culture. Younger students stayed on campus and explored unconventional curriculum options, such as bridge or yoga. Even parents were curious about what Dr. Marney might be teaching in her yearly sex education class.

Bigger, Better, Bursting at the Seams

As for the other major change in society, Harpeth Hall offered an excellent educational option for Nashville parents dissatisfied with the long bus rides and frequent changes of school created by Metro Nashville's busing plan, enacted in 1971.

Harpeth Hall had added seventh and eighth grades, the Daugh W. Smith Middle School, in 1968 and added a sixth grade in 1971. The 1975 freshman class, the first class subject to busing in 1971, was the largest in the school's history. The surge of interest in Harpeth Hall must have been a relief for the school's management and supporters, as interest in private, single-gender schools was dwindling elsewhere. "Coeducation" was the byword on campuses. Indeed, several boys' schools in the Nashville area would not see the end of the decade.

By 1973, the student body numbered 551, thirty-four of whom were children of alumnae, known as "legacies." The larger student body had the facilities bulging at the seams. For several years, classes were convened wherever there was a space large enough. Health classes were held in the basement of Souby Hall, known as the Mole Run. Other classes met in the conference room and in classrooms under the auditorium.

In 1975, the original auditorium was renovated into two floors of much needed classroom space. The floors were named the Louise Bullard Wallace Educational Wing. Ground was broken in 1976 for the auditorium/gymnasium/studio/gallery complex that would later be known as the McMurry Center for Arts and Athletics. The Center comprises the Frances Bond Davis Auditorium, Catherine E. Morrison Gymnasium and the Marnie Sheridan Gallery.

The new space changed the way things were done at Harpeth Hall. Physical education offerings had largely consisted of team sports, such as field hockey, tennis and basketball. The new athletic facility included studios that allowed for early aerobics-type classes called body dynamics and dance classes such as jazz, tap, modern and ballet. Girls who were not especially competitive suddenly had a whole new way to be physically active. With the Marnie Sheridan Gallery open, the school held an exhibit of the work by the first art teacher at Harpeth Hall, Lenora Litkenhous, in September 1977. A hugely popular alumnae art exhibit followed in the fall of 1978.

DR. DAUGH W. SMITH

Dr. Daugh W. Smith, a founder of Harpeth Hall and chairman of the board of trustees for 25 years, was one of the mainstays of the Harpeth Hall community from the first. When Dr. Smith retired as chairman in 1977, the trustees bestowed on him the title of Chairman Emeritus and life member of the board and awarded him the Dede Bullard Wallace Award for Distinguished Service to Harpeth Hall. His love for the school can still be seen on the campus. He had a special touch and a unique knowledge of growing things. He could literally call each tree, shrub and flower by name and personally supervised all planting and cultivation of the campus landscaping.

Dr. Smith was also a champion of education for young women. He was consistent in his efforts to keep Harpeth Hall an outstanding independent school for girls and played a leading role in each major building project on the campus: the Bullard Gymnasium and classroom addition in 1954; the Annie C. Allison Library in 1966; the Daugh W. Smith Middle School in 1968; the Wallace Wing in 1975; and the McMurry Center in 1977. His dream for many years had been a new science building to replace the crowded chemistry and biology laboratories and to provide space for the computer sciences. He also wanted an addition to the Middle School to accommodate the sixth grade classrooms. Both dreams were fulfilled after his death in 1983.

Dr. Smith's immeasurable gift of love and time to Harpeth Hall remain unequaled. As the plaque in the Daugh W. Smith Memorial Garden appropriately reads, "He did not count the hours."

THE DANCE PROGRAM

"When the McMurry Center was built, I went over there and met Miss McMurry. We talked for four hours," said Leslie Matthews (Mullins), who was employed to start Harpeth Hall's dance program in 1977. "You can credit her and Miss Patty with the decision to add dance to the curriculum. A girls' school is conducive to it. There were a lot of students who didn't want to do a team sport. But there was an increased interest in athleticism. It was a tremendous success. The first dance club meeting, I had 85 people show up."

Dance offered an opportunity for both personal expression for those not handy with pastels and good exercise, as well as lessons in posture and body control. For many young dancers, it was a way to exercise without participating in a competitive or team sport.

"I have very poor eye-hand coordination, and I'm not competitive," said Ms. Matthews. "The wonderful thing about dance is the only competition

is within yourself. Other people don't agree with that. But in my philosophy it's every dancer's journey." More than grace and athleticism, dance offers the world in a nutshell, Matthews believes. "I also think it teaches you life's lessons in a way. There's structure and beauty and discipline and guidelines for running your life. It's one of the reasons the arts are so important in an academic environment."

Besides teaching dance classes in the physical education department, Ms. Matthews was the dance club sponsor, putting on the spring dance concert for 22 years until, with mixed feelings, she handed over the spring 2000 concert to Tina Trinkler Cowlyn ('83), a former Harpeth Hall student.

For a year in the mid-'70s, the drama department performed in the cafeteria, putting on *The Crucible* and *You Can't Take it With You* among the tables and chairs. That ended with the new auditorium. *Cinderella* was the first musical done in the new space. *Blithe Spirit* was produced in the fall of 1978. *The Matchmaker* was the spring 1979 school production. The Montgomery Bell Academy and Harpeth Hall choruses teamed up for *Pirates of Penzance* in 1978. The first-ever student dance concert was held on the new stage in 1978. The better space and sound system made it possible for the school to bring in outside performers like Gene Cotton and Ray Stevens as well as better appreciate the singing talents of students like Amy Grant ('78), who frequently performed during assembly. While still a student at Harpeth Hall, Amy Grant released her first album, entitled *Amy Grant*.

Amy Grant performs at assembly

HARPETH HALL DANCE CLUBS

PRESENT

1978 SPRING CONCERT

FRIDAY, MAY 19th   8:00 P.M.

HARPETH HALL SCHOOL
DAVIS AUDITORIUM

Athletics Makes Strides

Women's athletics were expanding in the 1970s as traditional sports such as field hockey and half-court basketball fell out of favor and new ones such as aerobics and dance appeared. Before the school joined the city league (then called the NIL) in the mid-'70s, basketball rivals were limited to St. Cecilia, St. Bernard and independent girls' schools in Chattanooga and Memphis, remembers Beth Lewis Murphy ('71). "It seemed like Harpeth Hall didn't have many athletes. But we did! They were all playing on church teams," she says. And it's true that power players Cathy Dale McCain, Evelyn Byrd Blackmon, Susan Duvier Bass and Douglass Smith (all '73) played for the First Presbyterian team.

The school joined the Tennessee Secondary School Athletic Association in 1974. The previous year the association passed a rule that students could play either church basketball or school basketball, but not both. "I couldn't understand why our best players were playing church league instead of school. It's because that's where they had always played," says Murphy. The switch was made from half-court to full-court basketball. "It was hard-fought," says Pat Moran, physical education instructor and coach from 1956 to 1996. "The men who coached girls didn't want it. They didn't think the draw would be there for girls' basketball if they played like boys. The women wanted it. What finally turned the worm was the fact that Pat Summit [coach of women's basketball at University of Tennessee] said, 'I will not recruit a girl from Tennessee if she hasn't played full-court basketball.'"

Tennis enjoyed a gigantic surge in popularity in the 1970s. In pleasant weather, every tennis court in Nashville was full, and indoor courts were built for winter play. Harpeth Hall's own courts were very popular with the surrounding neighborhoods. Beginning in the early 1970s, the school fielded a series of dominant teams. On the strength of players like Laurie Copple Power ('76) , Grace Trammel ('75), Caroline McNeilly Bartholomew ('76) and Susan Bradley ('79), these teams won the NIL championship four years in a row between 1973 and 1976.

Begun in 1972, the track program had an impressive record by 1976. This was due in part to runner Margaret Groos Sloan ('77), a standout even among her talented teammates. She set a national record in the mile run at an Optimist meet at Overton High School during the 1974-75 year, clocking 4:59.05. She bested that time at the state championship with a time of 4:52.3. Harpeth Hall won the state track title that year. Following graduation, Groos set a world record in the indoor 5,000 meter run, and in 1988, she won the marathon at the U.S. Olympic Trials. English teacher Dr. Betty Marney shares this anecdote about Groos' impressive speed: "We had a water balloon attack from BGA students while I was there . . . She [Margaret] was sitting in Dorothea Griffin's math class. These guys came down the hall throwing water balloons. Margaret asked if she could chase them, and Dorothea agreed. They must have thought Wonder Woman was chasing them because she was so fleet of foot. They were scrambling to get in their truck. But they blew it because she got their license number."

In the late 1970s, Harpeth Hall simply dominated the track scene, taking district championships, regional runner-ups and state championships in cross country. Even the

Middle School excelled: in 1977-78, the Middle School track team was the HVAC champion. Field hockey was having its last varsity hurrah, as fewer and fewer nearby schools offered it. "We had varsity field hockey, but the only varsity we could play was Sewanee. For us to travel to the Northeast was not even an option. I remember one time going to Sewanee to play field hockey against a college team. We showed up in our kilts and they thought we were ready to play because you play hockey in kilts," recalls Susan Thornton ('76), who also won a state title in the shot put. Around the time field hockey was dropped in the late 1970s, volleyball slid in to take its place as a varsity sport.

Another tremendous student athlete was Tracy Caulkins Stockwell ('81), part of a winning swim team that never practiced together and had no pool. "Everyone was AAU. I remember we won the state meet because everyone on the team won their events," said teammate Jeanne Harris Broadwell ('79). Tracy was remarkably able to juggle her school work with a grueling four-hour-a-day, six-day-a-week practice schedule. She remarked, "That meant doing homework in the car, making the most of study hall. Basically it meant using your time wisely and being quite disciplined." Tracy won her first national title in 1977 and, in 1978, won five gold medals and one silver medal at the World Championships in Berlin. At the 1984 Olympics in Los Angeles, she won three gold medals. Miss Patty attended to cheer her on.

Real Role Models, Grand Characters

In the memories of students, the instructors and staff of Harpeth Hall were as much a cast of characters as they were instructors. The school was fortunate that the decade of change didn't much alter the composition of the faculty.

Mrs. Ottarson is the first name on many alumnae lips when asked about memorable teachers in the 1970s. Jencie Adams Tipton ('75) was in her Latin class, but she definitely remembered more about the shoes than the class. "Betsy Nesbitt, Debbie Davis and I would keep a running list of the shoes she wore and when she wore them," she says. "I think she had 100 or so pairs." Students found the varieties of shoes fascinating too: chartreuse Mary Janes and espadrilles decorated with tulips or daisies. "She'd get in that car and rev it up and smoke would pour out," says Lacy Jamison Nelson ('76). "All you could see when she 'took off' were her two gloved hands," wrote Mrs. Tipton.

Señor Pavia, a Spanish teacher in the Upper School, was another memorable figure for the girls. His courtly manners, dramatic accent, playful manner and petite frame were as memorable as his leisurely teaching style and apparently full social schedule. A Volkswagen owner, Pavia was one of only a handful of teachers to make it to school in the terrible snowstorm of January 1978. Another student recalled his bringing in corn cakes from Nero's Cactus Canyon, a Green Hills restaurant, to share with the class.

Students favored personable science teacher Betsy Malone and dedicated the 1974-75 yearbook to her as the senior class's sponsor. She was also a Winterim sponsor to marine biology camp in Big Pine Key around that time. Thus she was front and center in the public bus the group was riding when Winterim student Chris Woolwine Bettis ('77) grabbed the microphone and sang "Life is a Cabaret" to the other, doubtless astonished, riders. In 1998-99, Mrs. Malone was named director of the Middle School.

POLLY FESSEY (W-B '43) AND THE DAUGH W. SMITH MIDDLE SCHOOL

When Harpeth Hall decided to start a Middle School in 1968, Headmistress Idanelle McMurry called on her old Ward-Belmont and Vanderbilt classmate Polly Fessey to be head of the school. At the time, Miss Fessey was working with the Girl Scouts. She had worked as executive director of what is now the Cumberland Valley Girl Scout Council before moving to Memphis to work with the national staff of the Girl Scouts. It was at the 1968 Ward-Belmont reunion that Miss McMurry asked her to head up the new Middle School.

"We were starting from scratch. The first year we kind of learned as we went. We really approached it as a team . . . like 'We really have a wonderful opportunity here. Let's make the most of it,'" says Miss Fessey. The Middle School began with 140 students in seventh and eighth grades and a faculty of experienced teachers. "We felt our responsibility was to train girls for the Upper School, to instill in them the love of learning and to prepare them to make the best of their high school years," she adds.

Her biggest challenge, she says, was to create an atmosphere of learning and to make it an atmosphere that made it enjoyable to learn. "Pulling these two things together took a little doing," Miss Fessey remarks. "It was a happy atmosphere . . ."

Miss Fessey is remembered for her even-keeled, quiet approach to administration. "She was steadfast and supportive. She was there for you. She came to all the games," remembers Babs Young Behar ('79). She was also remembered for her dog, who is included in most of her yearbook portraits. Miss Fessey served as interim headmistress in 1979-80 following Miss McMurry's resignation. She then returned to the Middle School where she worked until her retirement in 1989.

From 1971 to 1974, some Middle School students were fortunate to take a class from renowned southern author Lee Smith (Seay), who taught seventh grade English and creative writing. Smith said, "I loved it. I believe in single-sex education because of the freedom it gives kids. It frees you up from your biology for a little bit of the day." She loved teaching young people, she says, "because when you're 12 years old, everything is new. Suddenly, they are often times having very adult vocabularies and intuitions and ideas." Smith's third novel, *Fancy Strut,* was published in 1973 while she was at Harpeth Hall.

Physical education instructor Mrs. Moran is remembered for encouraging athletics without being radical. She was the senior class sponsor in 1976, and they called her "Mom" Moran. Ginger Osborn [Justus] ('66) was hired in 1973 to teach the new philosophy class. An alumna herself and working on a doctorate, her own passion for intellectual stimulation set an example for her students.

Steve Kramer taught both American and advanced placement history and was thought by many students to be a dreamboat as well. "That good-looking Steve Kramer," summed up Karin Adams Barro ('77). "He was a smart, very effective teacher. He knew how to get his point across," says Alison Cunningham Anderson ('79). He required his students to read the Perspective section of the Sunday newspaper so they would be exposed to international news. He also coached a series of unstoppable track teams in the 1970s. Kramer was also

remembered for his sapphire blue Mazda RX-7. "He covered it every day," recalls Shelly Pearson Peterson ('79). In 1979, the students held an informal "Cover Your Car" day. "We all brought sheets and covered our cars."

Janet Hensley served the school for many years, teaching ancient history in the Middle School and later serving as dean of the Upper School. "I remember her smoking in the teachers' lounge," recalls Susan Thornton ('76). "I walked through the office one day, and she was leaning up against the radiator with a cigarette. I walked by and took it away. When she went to take a drag, there was nothing there," she laughed. Susan also recalled that Miss Hensley "was the best teacher I ever had. She just made you work and made you think." Anita Woodcock Schmid ('68) accepted a job offer to teach psychology from Headmistress Idanelle "Sam" McMurry on the same day she got a cat. "It had a white stripe on its head, so I named it Sam," she recalls.

Some instructors were loved just for being themselves: history teacher Violet Jane Watkins was an animated lecturer and avid birdwatcher. She brought her binoculars to class with her so as not to miss a single avian specimen. Patty Chadwell is remembered for her pleated skirt and crisp white shirt, rhythmics class and her tender concern for the George Washington birthday costumes. Study hall supervisor Germaine VanCleemput was recalled for her distinctive German accent. Betty Marney's quick wit, sharp tongue and expressive eyebrow captivated students, as did Dona Gower's extraordinary hair-do, ever-present shawl and glamorous lipstick.

Dr. Martha Overholser, like many legendary teachers, was both feared and admired. Many students recall that she gave two grades to each paper: one for composition and another for spelling. Woe betide the weak speller. She was awarded the Dede Bullard Wallace Award for outstanding service to the school in teaching in 1975. "I learned more about grammar, word usage, and vocabulary from her than from any other teacher before or since," says Lacy Jamison Nelson ('76).

At the close of the 1970s, Dr. Overholser surprised everyone by announcing that she would retire. "No one ever surprises me as much as myself. I am so wrapped up in my teaching that I never thought I'd ever want to quit!" she told the alumnae publication. The mystery was solved a few weeks later when she added that she would marry Dr. Laurence I.

AMERICAN FIELD SERVICE

The junior class fashioned a chapter of the American Field Service in 1971, with the aim of "turning places into people," wrote Lonnie Nelson Frey, the chapter's sponsor, by bringing foreign students to campus and sending Harpeth Hall students elsewhere. AFS students spending a year at Harpeth Hall included Paula Ripon from New Zealand, who was hosted by the Nelson Andrews family; Jane Gardiner from South Africa, a tennis enthusiast who spent the 1974-1975 academic year at the school, living with the Owsley Cheeks; and Rita Props, a Belgian student, hosted by the Rascoe Davis family. The school sent Beth Davis ('74) to Malaysia as its first AFS exchange student. Jac Reiners came from Germany for the 1975-1976 school year.

Sema Aygor from Turkey attended during the 1973-1974 academic year. Her host family, the family of Margaret Millis Faust ('74), attended her 1977 wedding in Turkey (interestingly, it was not an arranged marriage). Italian Alessandra Dechigi stayed with the Guv Pennington family in 1977-78. Like many Europeans, Alessandra was multilingual and politically far more sophisticated than American teenagers. She disliked skirts, so the school uniform was a challenge for her. On the other hand, she was delighted by the school's carpeted floors.

But the most distinctive of the AFS students was the first, Manely Ramirez-Abella, of La Plata, Argentina, who visited in 1970-1971. She lived with the family of Donna Tanner ('72). She was pretty and dimpled and came from a well-to-do family. When she returned to Argentina, she became politically active against the military junta. It was a bold step, because the government had a sinister way of handling citizen protest: they kidnapped and killed them. One estimate holds that one person on every block in every Argentine city "disappeared," and in fact that was the term for them: *los desaparacedos*.

Manely (pronounced muh-NELLI) kept in touch with the Tanners after she married. She knew her activism was dangerous. In a 1976 letter to the Tanners, she wrote, "If I die soon, I would like you to know how much I love you, what a wonderful time I had when I was part of the family . . . if something happens to me, please don't be sad because I chose this, and I'm happy because I fight for the happiness of all my people." She married and had a baby boy. When the baby was a few months old, on December 29, 1977, the whole family was kidnapped from their home. The parents were killed within days, but the baby turned up at the local police department in February and was raised by his grandparents.

Years later, in the early 1990s, a performance at a Harpeth Hall dance concert told Manely's story. "They had her face on their costumes," recalls Sue Fort White ('73). "They did an incredible piece about the oppression and that whole horrible time, and it was in memory of Manely."

Hewes, Jr. An even more profound personnel change also came in 1979 when Miss McMurry announced that she would leave Harpeth Hall for a post at Hockaday, a girls' preparatory school in Dallas. At commencement ceremonies that year, board of trust chair John S. Beasley II awarded Miss McMurry the Dede Bullard Wallace Award, saying to the graduates, "like you, she takes with her the sum of Harpeth Hall, and like you she leaves behind the aura of what she is, what she has accomplished, what she stands for." She was told that the new arts and athletics complex would henceforth bear her name. And finally, she was sent away with a gift of the times: a silver cigarette box.

Student Life in the Early 1970s

Conventional wisdom was that life at a girls' school was confining. But in fact, during a time like the 1970s, when it could be difficult to get one's bearings, a girls' school was liberating. At a girls' school, a young woman was just another student. There was an encouraging atmosphere in which to experiment with new ideas, new directions and new activities. The absence of boys made it possible to concentrate on studies and develop friendships. Probably it was just as well that there were no boys around because the rules of courtship and dating were changing. In the spirit of experimentation, Student Council President Susan Duvier Bass ('73) decided to try a little social engineering with the fall dance in 1972. The theme was Magical Mystery Tour. "I wanted girls that didn't have dates to come to the dance. I had a friend named Charles Flexner at Webb School in Bell Buckle, Tennessee. We arranged for a busload of boys from Webb," she remembers. "We thought it was going to be great, but it was miserable. Everyone was so self-conscious, and it was all so contrived. We renamed it Magical Misery Tour."

In 1974, the student council tried something else: sending blind invitations to men for the first (and only) Stags No Drag dance. After those two experiments, just calling a boy and asking him on a date seemed reasonably normal.

Middle School Combo 1971

On campuses all across the country, students were protesting. The protests were largely rooted in opposition to the Vietnam War, but they created an atmosphere in which protesting was increasingly accepted. Native Americans protested their mistreatment; Berkeley students seized vacant land for a people's park. And as the decade opened, Harpeth Hall got caught in the frenzy. Student Council President Beth Tanner ('70) wanted to abolish many of the school's institutions and traditions, such as the intramural clubs. "Miss McMurry said it was like a black cloud had come over Harpeth Hall because it was the beginning of all that protest. We'd have assemblies where they would play music on acoustic guitars and sing protest songs," says Susan Duvier Bass ('73).

In a lighter spirit, seniors held a protest in front of the Senior House in 1970. They gathered in the shape of a B+ to ask that final exams for seniors be waived if they had a B+ or better average. Their request was denied. As if the women's

movement, desegregation, the culture of protest, shifting standards and strange clothes weren't enough, the '70s also ushered in the era of drugs and alcohol. With the drinking age in Tennessee being 18 in the early 1970s, "people would go to TGI Friday's after school to meet their boyfriends," remembers Cathy Ellis Connery ('72). Indeed, it wasn't unusual to run into students in local bars such as the Cockeyed Camel, since many seniors were 18 years old, and plenty of 17-year-olds appeared to be 18. It was an era of lax attitudes toward teenage drinking at any rate, and requests for identification were uncommon.

Headmistress McMurry didn't recall drugs being much of a problem at Harpeth Hall, though it's certain students tried them on their own time. Miss McMurry said the drug situation in the 1970s was largely "something I could fight because it was really rare."

Girls Just Want to Have Fun

The 1976 George Washington Birthday Celebration was a particularly big deal—the year of America's bicentennial. Because the class of '79 was so large, it added tableaux to the traditional lineup of birthday events. One was a short skit depicting young George's childhood, and another illustrated his successes as general.

Bake sales raged on and on as a great way to raise money among a perpetually hungry student body. One year the bake sale was supplanted by a sale of Reese's peanut butter cups to raise money for the new auditorium. Other interesting fund raisers during the decade included a Ms. Harpeth Hall contest in '74 and '75 (the winner wore a stole made of kilts); an antique car auction in 1977; and a charity horse show in 1978.

The Senior House got a soft drink machine in 1977, which Elizabeth Wright Ralph ('77) called one of the most memorable things that happened during her time at the school. "Everything was in bottles. The diet Dr. Pepper was the most popular thing. I reloaded the Coke machine. I kept the key on my kilt pin," she said.

Lunch remained the high point of every day in every student's life. In 1975, the favored meal was crackers with ice cream. "We RAN to lunch and then we would only eat fries and crackers," remembers Betsy Settle Brittain ('76). "The Belle Meade Cafeteria food was awful, yet everyone would run to be first in line." The

THE GREAT FRUIT FLY CAPER, JUNIOR-SENIOR DAY 1977

In the words of Dr. Marney, as a prank on Junior-Senior Day, junior Deborah Ezell Denson ('78) parked her Volvo sedan and blocked the access to the senior parking lot. "Someone came flying into my class talking about it. I went down there and sure enough that car was sitting there. I was told Deborah was in Spanish with Mr. Pavia. Phyllis Pennington leaned out the window and told us there were some fruit flies available from the lab. We hastily put the plan together. I knocked (on the door of Mr. Pavia's class) and asked to speak to Deborah. 'Give me your keys,' I said. She kept saying she would move the car herself, but I wasn't about to get her out there. I used a horribly stern voice and told her to sit down and study. She felt she was in trouble.

"The fruit flies were put into the car, and the car was driven elsewhere on the campus. It being a nice warm day, the fruit flies did what fruit flies do.... Deborah came outside at the end of class, and she was ballistic. Janet Hensley said that Deborah was using a series of unsavory and unladylike words. Sam (McMurry) was out of town. When she came back the next Monday, she was in the faculty lounge, and she said, 'I hear there was an incident on Junior-Senior day.' And I said, 'No, Deborah Ezell just got outpranked.'"

vogue that year was to eat the crackers with Thousand Island dressing. It was the age of dieting, and every 100 calories counted. Egg and prune diets were unaccountably popular, as was the Stillman Water Diet. Adelaide Davis Stevens ('79) confirms that by the end of the decade, the lunch menu was "Tab and crackers."

Many students will always remember the day in mid-decade when a neighborhood boy stripped off his clothes, donned a stocking cap for anonymity and "streaked" across the Harpeth Hall campus. "The teachers had to peel us off the windows," recalls Adelaide Davis Stevens ('79).

Cafeteria Staff

The More Things Change . . .

With the war over, integration achieved, environmental issues on the table and women in control of their child-bearing and moving into the workplace, the youthful drive to change the world had dramatically diminished. As the

decade drew to a close, it was as if the early 1970s had never happened. Gone were the floaty fashions and peasant duds that made a statement; the clothes long worn by prep school students were in vogue everywhere. Toga parties, rather than activism, had become the rage. A social reformer was supplanted in the Oval Office by an actor. Even the 1979 *Milestones* seemed to have amnesia stating: "It seems time changes nothing at Harpeth Hall; the ivy and trees merely grow a little taller and the lions a bit more tarnished."

The theme song of a junior class play at the end of the decade really says it all: "Be Young, Be Foolish, But Be Happy." At the close of the decade, it seemed like a worthwhile goal.

1980s

A TIME OF PROMISE

While the 1980s were at times fraught with uncertainty due to the attempt on President Reagan's life, the Iran hostage crisis and the explosion of the space shuttle Challenger, the overall imprint the '80s left was one of promise. "Tear down that wall" were the words heard around the globe as President Reagan called for a climactic end to the Berlin Wall. The boom of the personal computer and the Internet signaled unprecedented advances in information and technology and paved the way for a global economy.

The 1980s proved particularly dynamic for women. The groundwork laid in the 1960s and 1970s was being realized as doors opened up for young women, who were finally able to recognize their full potential as contributors to their community, their families and their world.

Harpeth Hall welcomed the technological and global age with a wide variety of initiatives felt throughout the student and faculty population. The school witnessed advances in curriculum, buildings and grounds and athletic facilities. It also experienced changes in faculty and staff, in traditions and in the way it related to the community at large. Throughout it all, Harpeth Hall continued to provide a nurturing, safe environment where young women could grow academically, artistically and personally, developing leadership and life skills that would carry them on to great achievements. It was indeed an exciting time to be at Harpeth Hall.

The Building Boom

For Harpeth Hall students in the '80s, there were always some new and exciting changes taking place on campus. Sometimes, it was as simple as the entrance, "or is that the exit now? No, I think they changed it back to the entrance last week!" at Hobbs Road changing…or the renovation of the original library in Souby Hall which had since been divided into offices and was now transformed into the

Bear Lair 1986

memorabilia-filled Ward-Belmont Room. In 1984 the study hall was refurbished and christened the Bear Lair—a favorite hangout for students during free time.

By the fall of 1984, Little Harpeth became a thing of the past, paving the way for the new Massey Center for Mathematics and Science. Gone were the old biology and chemistry labs and those great cubbyholes. Because of the ongoing construction, sunbathing was strictly prohibited that year. By the beginning of the next school year, the Math and Science Center with state-of-the-art classrooms and science labs was finally completed . . . and the sunbathing ban was lifted.

Dorothy Cate Frist and granddaughter Corinne Frist

The 1985-86 school year also saw the addition of the new sixth grade building to the Daugh W. Smith Middle School. Dorothy Cate Frist Hall was dedicated on October 3, 1985. Mari-Kate Hopper ('92) said, "I was in the last sixth grade class ('85-86) to be under the library and the first class to use Frist Hall. What a vast difference!"

A campaign began in 1983 to provide funds for the Math and Science Center and Frist Hall and also included $1 million for the endowment and plans for expanded athletic facilities. In May 1987 fund raising continued for these athletic facilities, and, in October 1987, Harpeth Hall hosted its first one-hour fun run, "Run for the Green," involving students, faculty, parents, alumnae and trustees. Proceeds from this successful event were used for landscaping for the new facility. More than spirits were "razed" during construction of the track, however. Several Indian graves estimated at 600-800 years old were almost bulldozed, but were respectfully and carefully moved to another site. Also in the fall of 1987, the new Patty Chadwell Tennis Courts were dedicated to the endearing Miss Patty, who retired in 1981 after being involved in practically every facet of the school's operations since it opened.

LEIGH HORTON GARDEN

A very special place on campus was dedicated on May 19, 1985—the Leigh Horton Garden. Originally the Ward-Belmont Garden, the beautifully landscaped Leigh Horton Garden features a sculpture of a young girl reading a book and a fountain bearing a plaque inscribed with, "For every joy that passes, something beautiful remains." A gazebo in the center of the garden provides a spot for students and faculty to spend quiet moments. Leigh Horton passed away in 1984 after a long battle with cancer. She would have graduated in 1985.

1966-1984

On the occasion of her death, English teacher Tom Young wrote the following poem:

We met stretched out and dozing in the grass
Your best friends baffled, absent, going dot
  To dot.
The sun was on us all, only heavier
On the flesh we wanted you to have. In
  "My Last Duchess"
We read of pert Lucrezia, dead at seventeen,
Locked in a body not her own.
I know I have never taught so well
As thinking what Lucrezia might have been
And of this one old world you would see
  Only today.
Afterwards, when you needed to rest
And were proud to say 'Ask me about the Duchess,'
Something bloomed and broke inside of me.

Attracting the Best

Harpeth Hall has always been fortunate to attract those special teachers who truly loved the art and philosophy of teaching as well as staff and administrators who took pride in seeing how the students grew over the years. While the school said good-bye to some of its favorite faculty members, it also welcomed new staff during this decade. The 1980s

began with a change in leadership. In 1980, David E. Wood was appointed the new headmaster. Hilrie Brown took over as admissions director in 1986. Jane Berry Jacques ('72) began as college counselor and dean of students in 1982. In 1989, Lindy B. Sayers took over the helm as head of the Middle School following Polly Fessey's retirement.

The most dramatic faculty change occurred in March of 1984 when several teachers simultaneously resigned in protest of a still-talked-about administrative decision. Mistakes were made by all the parties involved, and philo-

sophical differences kept people at odds. It was one of the darker moments for Harpeth Hall, and one that changed the face of the school for several years. In the end, though, the school is bigger than any one individual, and the loss of sev-

eral outstanding teachers ultimately paved the way for a new faculty with a new commitment to Harpeth Hall, its students and its mission.

In 1981 the men's club initiated a tradition of faculty appreciation by presenting Harpeth Hall chairs to selected faculty and staff who set an outstanding example. Currently, Faculty Appreciation Day recognizes the recipients of the coveted named, endowed chairs.

Faculty Appreciation Day

DAVID E. WOOD

David Wood, who joined Harpeth Hall in 1980 after serving 15 years as director of admissions at Vanderbilt and a four-year stint at all-male UMS preparatory school in Mobile, Alabama, says one of his guiding principles is "do what you are good at." For Wood, that means connecting with students. "I was always into sports so showing up for their games was something I liked to do, and it helped me get to know the parents as well as the students," Wood says. During the 11 years he was at Harpeth Hall, he figures he attended several hundred volleyball games, track meets, plays and basketball games. "I tried to go to all the events to show my support for the girls," explains Wood. "For me, the nicest thing a student can say is, 'Thanks for coming.'"

Wood was also good at maintaining and developing other programs that benefited students at the school. "I inherited a wonderful school," he says. "We just implemented a few changes and additions to the program to make it an even better school. Among the programs that he enhanced were the theatre program and the Harpeth Hall chorus. Attendance at all performances was record-breaking, and he also initiated two summer all-school community plays, *My Fair Lady* and *The Music Man,* which played to packed audiences.

In the area of student support, he started the Key Club to increase student involvement in community service and inaugurated the Father-Daughter Banquet and the annual college tour. He also created a room for the students, which he named the Bear Lair. All of these additions are still in place today. In the academic area, Wood was instrumental in obtaining the Morehead Scholarship nomination to the University of North Carolina for Harpeth Hall. Nomination for the Morehead Scholarship, which covers all college expenses, is open to only two schools in Tennessee. Cey Gray ('83) was the first student from Harpeth Hall to be awarded this prestigious scholarship. Wood also introduced computer classes that were very popular with the students. Strengthening of the math and science departments encouraged many students to continue with math and science classes for all four years of high school.

During his tenure, Wood increased the number of male faculty members and hired some exceptional young, talented classroom teachers. "Because so many girls lived in homes where there was no male presence, they needed some male role models," he explained. In addition, he raised funds to establish an endowment for professional development and enrichment for the faculty.

In 1981, one year after his arrival, Wood established the school's development program by putting in place the first full-time director of development. This program set the stage to launch a $3 million capital campaign in 1983 to secure funds to build the Mathematics and Science Center, now the Jack C. Massey Center, an addition to the Middle School, Dorothy Cate Frist Hall and $1 million for the endowment. Later, in 1987, a second campaign was initiated to build an eight-lane 400-meter track with a soccer field enclosed, a field house, and two softball fields.

Wood believes his greatest accomplishment at Harpeth Hall may be in making the school environment a happier place for students. While there, he learned every girl's name and became familiar with her interests. He had a special talent for helping a girl find her "niche," resulting in increased self-esteem and school spirit among the students. And, he made a real effort to be accessible to students, faculty and parents alike. His office door was open to all.

In 1990, Wood left Harpeth Hall to become the principal of the upper school at Pace Academy in Atlanta and to be near his ailing mother. In 1995, he became headmaster at St. Andrew's Episcopal School in Jackson, Mississippi. When he and Margie, his wife of 41 years, have time to reminisce, they agree that their 11 years at Harpeth Hall were special to them. He once wrote, "The first day I stepped on the campus as headmaster of Harpeth Hall, I felt this was a very special place. The years have served to reinforce and strengthen this feeling."

The Art of Teaching

Parlez-vous Français? Students did, thanks to Libby Evans, Barbara Carden, Bill Lauderdale, and Paul Tuzeneu. Diana Cherry ('85) looked back fondly on Libby Evans saying, "Mrs. Evans was demanding and expected much of her students. No English could be spoken in her classroom; she had no patience for laziness or misbehavior. It was obvious she 'knew her stuff,' and she was always fair. She was incredibly enthusiastic and quick to smile. It was in her class that

Libby Pope Evans

I came to love the idea of knowing a second language . . . I am still saddened that she died at such an early age because I know that she would have influenced those around her no matter what she chose to do." [*Editor's Note:* In 1987 Libby Evans succumbed to cancer. The Elizabeth Pope Evans award, given to the student in each class with the highest level of academic achievement, was established in her memory.]

Wende Hall Stambaugh ('85) recollects, "Like the children in *The Lion the Witch and the Wardrobe*, I walked into the 'wardrobe' of Tom Young's classroom and found a deeper, richer world of literature. No longer was I expected to respond by rote to a teacher's interpretation but pressed, cajoled and inspired to find for myself meaning and truth in each literary work. Like the magical world in C.S. Lewis' classic, I began to believe in myself, think for myself, take risks and eventually choose English as my

DOUBLE, DOUBLE TOIL AND TROUBLE

Harpeth Hall's three "witches"—English teachers Dr. Marney, Dr. Gower and Joan Warterfield—annually recited MacBeth's "double, double toil and trouble" speech, much to the delight of their students. The three "witches" were part of Harpeth Hall's English department in the early 1980s, which also included Louise Douglas Morrison (W-B '36), Sarah Stamps, Tom Young, Dugan Davis, Betty Latham Nelson (W-B '47) and Joyce Lee. How many girls ever made an automatic "F" for having a fragment or run-on sentence in a paper? If a student did it once, she never did it again, thanks to the foundation laid early by the Middle School English teachers. Those who were lucky to have one or more of these teachers have had their lives enriched and will never forget or underestimate the impact these teachers had. As Lisa Rudolph Turner ('80) sums up the fondness students had for their teachers, "Mrs. Stamps' class was a lesson in self-expression. She taught us not to be afraid to explore our feelings and put them on paper. She was so animated and full of life . . . I was a journalism major, probably thanks in part, to her."

minor at Sewanee." Anne Shoulders ('83) says, "Betty Nelson allowed me to write and think 'my way' as a young sixth grade student. Creative thinking is a skill I continued to develop over the years based on the foundation she gave me, and I depend on it daily as a marketing executive."

CELEBRATING **104** MILESTONES

A Time of Promise

Anyone who ever had Latin teachers Joyce Crutcher Ward ('60) or Phoebe Drews knew that *Roma in Italia est*, and *Amo, Amas, Amat, Amamus, Amatis, Amant*. Martha Gregory and Mary Lee Mathews Manier (W-B '42) knew where every book in the library was and provided indispensable assistance for research papers. Heidi Wallace Sanford ('83) recalls the impact eighth grade history teacher Elaine Simpson had on her life, "Mrs. Simpson was the toughest teacher I ever had. Because she challenged me, I learned to love and appreciate art history to this very day."

On the arts front, Ray Berry and Sandra Davis taught us how to sing "gleefully" and give a well-delivered speech in public. Sheila Morris Mohr ('85) remarks, "One of my all-time favorite classes was art with Peter Goodwin. What an awesome four years I had with him and I really felt like he brought out the budding artist in me. I remember enjoying my two years of AP Art—those classes were two periods long so you could really 'check out' and go deep into whatever masterpiece you were creating at the time—oh, so much fun!" In the early '80s, the dance clubs led by Leslie Matthews expanded, adding a ballet club taught by Stephanie Hamilton. The annual Spring Dance Concert that showcased the hard work of the dedicated students and teachers became a tradition unlike any other.

A beloved member of the maintenance staff from 1984 to 1994 was Fred Tindall. He was told that his job was to "take care of the teachers and the students." Affectionately known as "Mr. Fred," he says now that he misses the kids more than anything else. "They respected me. If I told them they couldn't do something, like at a dance, they would listen to me. They made me feel part of the school—like they were MY kids."

Hitting the Books

The 1984 retirement of founding staff member Lucile McLean, finance director and former typing teacher, prophetically coincided with the end of manual typing classes and the ushering in of computer classes. Technology had entered the curriculum to prepare students as they ventured into the world outside Harpeth Hall.

By the end of the decade, the Upper School had grown to include 67 different courses. In addition to the traditional science curriculum, students could take botany and ecology and their AP counterparts. Great Works became the first cross-disciplinary class, taught in rotation by members of the English department, and was offered to juniors and seniors

WINTERIM

By 1985, when Emily Fuller succeeded Janet Hensley as head of Winterim, the program was in need of a change that reflected the way the school and student's needs and expectations had changed. Students still had a choice of several light-hearted classes, valuable electives and trips abroad, but by 1987 there were some required courses. Students could choose courses in the areas of law and government, medicine, advertising and media, student teaching, business and merchandising and special education. Remembering Winterim, JoAnna Warnock Blauw ('83) reflects, "My junior year I took the Introduction to the Music Industry class. We spent a lot of time on Music Row visiting recording studios, record companies, radio and television stations, and I ended up with an internship at Opryland Productions. Those experiences definitely shaped my career choice and let me know what to expect and not to be intimidated, and my first job out of college was working for The Judds and went on to work with such greats as Conway Twitty, Randy Travis and George Jones."

Winterim 1985—Berlin Wall

in preparation for the AP English exams. Other areas that saw a significant amount of growth were the history and social science departments. By the 1988-89 school year, six courses were offered in the social sciences. Interest in these electives was way up thanks to the efforts and talents of golf club-wielding Department Chair Dr. Art Echerd. His Model United Nations and Youth Legislature were the stars of this ever-broadening department.

The demanding curriculum and the hard work it took to master one's studies obviously paid off for many students in the 1980s. On average, every class in the '80s boasted 20 or more National Merit semi-finalists and/or finalists. On a similar note, virtually every student eligible to take an AP exam did, and over 90 percent of those students scored a three or better.

Harpeth Hall graduates have attended more than 200 different colleges and universities around the country thanks in part to the college trips, initiated in 1980 by David Wood. These trips gave students first-hand experience and knowledge about prospective colleges. Angie Elson Fuller ('83) remembers, "One

Spring Break Trip to Washington, D.C.

thing I took away from that college trip was getting a feel for different kinds of colleges. Seeing so many different kinds of schools really helped me make my final decision about academics, school size, geographic location, etc. Plus, being on that bus with everybody, away from home, was a blast!"

Brains and Brawn

As with every aspect of Harpeth Hall, the 1980s saw a change in the available athletic opportunities with the demise of some sports and the birth of new ones. Field hockey became a sport of the past at Harpeth Hall in the 1970s and gave way to the soccer craze. In 1980 when Dugan Davis began the soccer program in the Upper School, there were no other girls' high school soccer teams, and so the varsity soccer team played college teams in addition to regular youth leagues. "Playing on that first varsity soccer team was

an incredible experience. If memory serves me correctly, we not only played Vanderbilt and Alabama—I believe we beat Alabama. We thought we were invincible, and we were so proud," says Jane Mabry Jackson ('82). Things continued to prosper for the varsity soccer team, and in 1985, under Coach Gordon Turnbull's direction, the varsity soccer team

advanced to the state championships for the first time. The Middle School soccer team flourished, too, winning HVAC championships in 1983 and 1986.

Cross country and track have always been some of Harpeth Hall's best and most popular sports, and the '80s were no different. Runners started off the decade with All-American cross country star, Sloan Burton ('81), who helped lead the Honeybears to NIL, regional and state titles in 1980 and 1981. The winning tradition

continued in 1982 with Coach Susan Russ being named NIL Coach of the Year and again in 1984 when they went undefeated and were NIL Champs. The Middle School made its mark in 1986 by winning the HVAC Championship. In 1980, the varsity track team took first place in the TSSAA Division AA in the region and the state. In 1983 it was the Middle School's turn to shine, taking the HVAC title.

In 1982 and 1983 the varsity tennis team posted undefeated seasons in district play. In 1984, Diana Cherry ('85) and Elizabeth Arnold ('84) captured second place in the state doubles tennis championship. In 1985, Mary Lauren Barfield Allen ('88) and Buffy Baker ('87) placed first in state singles. In 1986, the varsity tennis team won its first-ever state championship, and in 1987 the Middle School tennis team won the HVAC Championship. As in seemingly every sport at Harpeth Hall, the varsity tennis team wrapped up the decade in 1989 with District and Regional Championships.

Playing on that first varsity soccer team was an incredible experience . . .
We thought we were invincible, and we were so proud.
—Jane Mabry Jackson ('82)

Under the direction of Nan Reed, the golf team captured the TSSAA regional lowest combined score in 1982 and 1983, thanks to the efforts of golfers Debbie Sheffield Bryan ('83) and Lil Bradford Smith ('84). In 1988, Linden Wiesman ('93) qualified for the All-State Tournament.

Riflery started in 1984 under the direction of Emmons Woolwine, and in this sport, Harpeth Hall competed with MBA, David Lipscomb and other all-male teams. By the 1987-88 school year softball became an official sport in the Upper School and was coached by Tony Springman. In 1989 the softball teams christened their new ballparks and finally had their own home field advantage. Girls celebrated their athletic feats with an end-of-the-year banquet, which in 1986 became a Dessert Fest. In 1988, the Emmons Woolwine Award, established in memory of the riflery coach who died earlier in the year, was awarded to the senior who exemplified kindness, loyalty and dedication in any sport.

STUDENT COUNCIL

In addition to representing the student body and its concerns to faculty and administration, the student council showed the student body a good time. Student council members did this through the annual Upper School Fall Dance and the Spring Dance, Dud's Days, surprise outings for the whole student body and the Harpeth Hall/MBA Square Dance, which started in 1981, to name a few. For many years the Spring Dance's theme was Hawaiian Holiday, but by the mid-'80s the theme began to change from year to year. In 1985, the student council undertook a new project by opening the Bear Necessities, a student-run bookstore in Souby Hall. In 1986, the student council started another new tradition with the Concert on the Lawn which was a super-sized picnic and field day, the Back-to-School Submarine Party in August and the Holiday Dance every December with the help of the Mothers' Auxiliary. The student council wasn't all fun and games, though. They took part in several student council exchanges and the AAA Conferences, designed to discuss academics, athletics and arts, with other private schools in Tennessee like GPS, Hutchison, Baylor and McCallie. In 1981 and again in 1989, a special student council exchange with MBA allowed members of each student council to attend classes at the other school for a day. Talk about seeing how the other half lives?!

Tradition-al Twist

Harpeth Hall Honor Day in the Middle School and graduation in the Upper School have always been steeped in tradition. Step Singing on the front lawn of Souby Hall and graduation on the front steps of the library have been long-standing traditions. Only once in the 1980s—for the class of 1986—did graduation have to be moved to the gym due to bad weather.

In 1985, then Senator Al Gore, Jr. was the guest speaker, but he had more than graduates, family and friends to address. That was the year of the cicada, and they were everywhere. Students recalled that the cicadas were so loud and thick that you could barely hear the speakers above the chirping! Senator Gore, however, was undeterred despite being 45 minutes late for the ceremony! After that year, and not because of the cicadas or Senator Gore, Harpeth Hall started a new tradition of choosing a graduation speaker from within the senior class. That was also the last year that Harpeth Hall held a Baccalaureate ceremony, with Sarah Ophelia Colley Cannon (Minnie Pearl) (W-B '32) addressing the graduates. In 1987, Step Singing took place in front of the library rather than Souby Hall.

Graduation 1981

Another unique tradition that was altered in the 1980s was the annual George Washington Birthday Celebration. In 1981 the honor and responsibility for performing this age-old celebration passed from the freshmen to the seventh grade class. Merrie Morrisey Clark ('69), Middle School history teacher, assumed the responsibility for this unique celebration from Miss Patty. Because of the switch, a Harpeth Hall fast fact will always be that the class of 1984 was the only one never to have participated in this tradition since it was established at the school in 1954.

The four clubs—Angkor, Ariston, Eccowasin and Triad—had been an integral part of student life at Harpeth Hall. However, as a result of response from a student and faculty poll organized by faculty member Ginger Osborn [Justus] ('66), the four clubs were combined into two clubs, the ArTris and the AnEccos starting in the fall of 1981, in order to boost participation and enthusiasm for club events. Club events were then divided into two categories: intramurals and challenges. In a 1981 *Logos II* (the student newspaper) article, reporter Jessica Ward McCarroll ('83) documented the first challenge held—a bicycle race: "Both teams were even until AnEccos' Sarah Nichols ran into a tree when her bike went out of control. The AnEccos' misfortune was increased when this reporter hit a bump and flew over the handlebars. After several teachers voiced concern the race was stopped . . . Mrs. Justus suggested they use big wheels next time."

The annual All-Club Picnic every May was a time for the clubs to show their spirit, compete for Best Club Song and for the school to hand out a variety of citizenship, athletic and club awards. By 1985 the club intramural system was overhauled as participation waned,

and in 1986 the first Awards Day took place. Awards Day was a new twist on the old All-Club Picnic theme, with class song competition, club awards presentations, installation of new student council officers and the announcement of Lady of the Hall. Another first happened at that first Awards Day—Carol Cavin ('86) was named Lady of the Hall and also received the Katie Wray Award. Despite the evolution of the four original clubs and the All-Club Picnic into Awards Day, and then the rebirth of the four clubs and All-Club Picnic in 1989, the outcome was the same: students came together for friendly competition, to say good-bye, to recognize each other for outstanding accomplishments and to look back over another year at Harpeth Hall.

Meanwhile, in the Middle School the four clubs and the sixth grade Greyhounds and Greenie-Meanies remained strong and engaged in community projects every year. Projects included everything from stuffing Christmas stockings for the Salvation Army and sponsoring a clothing drive to volunteering at the Harris-Hillman Friendship Fair for handicapped children.

Another tradition that got a new look was Senior Recognition Day, which always culminated with the senior class introducing its class song and class colors and being presented with their class beanies. The class of 1987 put its own spin on tradition by choosing "Gilligan" hats instead of beanies and then again the class of 1989 chose visors. Another tradition that began in the 1980s was the annual Father-Daughter Banquet, which started in 1981 and was sponsored by the men's club.

STEPPIN' OUT

The Junior/Senior Prom is a long-standing tradition at Harpeth Hall. Juniors work tirelessly for weeks making preparations and decorating the gym so that everything is perfect for the seniors. The 1981 Junior/Senior Prom started the tradition of the students electing a Prom Queen: Charlotte Booth Maguire ('81) was the first.

1980 French Promenade
1981 Celebration!
1982 On Broadway
1983 Here's Looking at You
1984 Mardi Gras
1985 Midsummer Night's Dream
1986 Shangri-la
1987 Magic Carpet Ride
1988 Underwater Fantasy
1989 Mystical Mirage

Student Life

There was more to life at Harpeth Hall than books and extracurricular activities. Students, and especially seniors, rocked to the sounds of "new wave" and Duran Duran, R.E.M. and U2 and saw the creation of MTV and Madonna. Seniors were glued to the television as the sagas of Luke and Laura, Jenny and Gregg, Bo and Hope, and Roman and Marlena unfolded in the afternoon—after classes, of course.

Students also had the opportunity to participate in a myriad of new clubs and activities that were born in the 1980s. Leadership retreats, college trips, Key Club, Quill & Scroll, Club Fair and other academic clubs have now become part of the Harpeth Hall culture. Even the uniform underwent a change—instead of saddle oxfords, students were allowed to wear penny loafers! Joanna Rutter, director of the Upper School, initiated Senior Dress-up Day in the 1983-84 school year. The first Friday of the month, seniors were allowed to be out of uniform. By 1985 this day had grown to include off-campus lunches, thanks to Betsy Turnbull, who became Upper School director following Mrs. Rutter's departure.

In 1980, David Wood started the leadership retreat. Club presidents, class presidents, student and honor council presidents, and faculty sponsors spent an August weekend in Camp Hy-Lake that first year. The theme was Leadership 1980 and was designed to educate the leaders of the clubs on parliamentary procedure and effective leadership skills. Over the years the theme of the retreat has evolved to include informative discussions and organizational planning as well as adding more student representatives.

Freshmen retreats also started in 1983, and the highly anticipated eighth grade trips started in 1985 when Latin

> *The Honor Council . . .*
> *acts as a reminder to the*
> *students of the importance*
> *of personal honor.*
> *—Ruthie Frederiksen DeRosa ('85)*

teacher Joyce Crutcher Ward ('60) took a small group to Chicago. By the late '80s this trip had evolved into an annual pilgrimage to Dauphin Island, Alabama that was a requirement of all eighth graders.

The Honor Council, one of the most important organizations at Harpeth Hall, began in 1980. Students had always been required to sign the pledge at the end of their work, but in 1980, a formal board of students and faculty was formed to ensure that the pledge was upheld and to deal with any violations of the honor code. Ruthie Frederiksen DeRosa ('85), former Honor Council president, said, "The Honor Council is a vital part of Harpeth Hall, for not only does it serve to uphold the honor system, it more importantly acts as a reminder to the students of the importance of personal honor."

THE PLAY'S THE THING

Playmakers Musical and Dramatic Productions and Middle School Musicals:

1979-80   The Sound of Music / Arsenic & Old Lace / Hobbit

1980-81   Oklahoma! / The Night of January 16th / Wizard of Oz

1981-82   My Fair Lady / Oliver / The Curious Savage /
Wind in the Willows

1982-83   South Pacific / Ten Little Indians / Velveteen Rabbit

1983-84   The Music Man / No, No Nanette /
You Can't Take it With You / Cinderella

1984-85   Anything Goes / Bull in a China Shop /
Alice in Wonderland

1985-86   Oklahoma / Ladies of the Jury / Wizard of Oz

1986-87   Carnival / The Madwoman of Chaillot /
Hobbit

1987-88   Mame / Pride & Prejudice /
How to Eat Like a Child

1988-89   42nd Street / Masterpieces / Snoopy

Arsenic & Old Lace

In 1980, the Nashville Kiwanis Club chartered the Key Club, whose primary function is to serve as a community service club. In its first four years it was named the most outstanding Key Club in its division and went on to sponsor such community outreach programs as the annual blood drive and used book sale. The Outing Club also started in 1980 and

Key Club 1986

provided an opportunity for students to take trips and go on school-sponsored adventures. Over the years students have been seen rafting down the Ocoee, bicycling around Radnor Lake and spelunking in Mammoth Cave.

What did Harpeth Hall girls eat for lunch every day? In the 1980s the traditional meat-and-three hot meal changed to include a hamburger and

hot dog bar, a salad bar and the ubiquitous student council candy bar sales that were held until 1983-84. If you forgot your lunch on a particular day each spring, you were in luck if it was the same day as the Senior Lunch Auction, begun in 1981.

Seniors used their imaginations to come up with themes for exquisite lunches to be auctioned off during assembly to an individual or a group. Students dug deep into their pockets and often bid $40 or $50 for a $5 lunch!

The 1986-87 school year saw the start of the Club Fair in which the various clubs on campus set up booths in the

Bear Lair and enthusiastically tried to solicit members. That same year, Harpeth Hall introduced Chemical Awareness Week, which evolved into Students Thinking Straight in 1988. This undertaking showed a highly developed sense of personal responsibility and caring for others that could only have grown and thrived in an environment such as Harpeth Hall. The purpose of this organization was to provide drug-and alcohol-free outings for students as well as education about the dangers of chemical substances. MBA offered a similar program, and the two clubs went on a variety of joint outings.

The Debate Club also made a comeback in 1983 at the urging of English teacher Gordon Turnbull; he was also responsible for the birth of the Quiz Bowl the following year.

A New Day Dawning

As the 1980s drew to a close, Harpeth Hall students were reflecting on the changes that had taken place in the school, the community and the world. The 1988 *Milestones* noted the importance of studying and understanding the changes and juxtaposing the old traditions with the new ones, saying in its opening, "Knowledge of the school's history will help students understand certain aspects of this annual." Indeed, students in the '80s undoubtedly remember something about each year that shaped their lives, but despite being such a dynamic decade full of milestones, the 1980s was just one part of the whole that made Harpeth Hall's first 50 years unforgettable.

CINDY CRIST ART COLLECTION AND AWARD

Cindy Crist ('85) died tragically the summer after her graduation from Harpeth Hall. Cindy was an artist of singular talent. As a memorial, family members, classmates and friends established a fund for the Cindy Crist Art Purchase Award. A painting is purchased each year from the outstanding senior class artist and becomes part of the Cindy Crist Art Collection which is on exhibit in the lobby of the Massey Center.

1990s

A NEW IDENTITY

The 1990s were a time of renewal and recommitment for Harpeth Hall as it strived to stay current with the needs of today's young women. Women not only desired to have the same education as men but to have one in which their differences, their interests and their dreams were taken into account. The school had seen the world around it explode with news of the Gulf War, the Oklahoma City bombings and the Clinton scandal. Though at times the ivory tower of academia had been punctured with deaths and crises, the community of Harpeth Hall always responded with characteristic strength and grace. As European history teacher Dr. Art Echerd recalls, "I remember events that never made local headlines, like the time when a junior, Ashley Smith ('99), almost lost her life in a series of very prolonged operations, and the school, in a gesture of solidarity, held a blood drive in which virtually every member of the Harpeth Hall community old enough to give blood did so." Though Nashville has grown exponentially as a city with the influence of professional sports, healthcare and big industry, Harpeth Hall has never lost its sense of community nor its vision of what a woman's education should be.

Massey Center Dedication 1991

Growth of a Campus

In the '90s Harpeth Hall grew not only in enrollment but physically as well, as facilities on campus were upgraded and new buildings were erected. The Middle School perhaps changed the most, with the addition of a state-of-the-art seventh grade science lab completed in 1994 and the Melkus Science Center, a new eighth grade science lab created in 1996 from existing Middle School space. The cafeteria was completely renovated in 1999 and named the Ingram Dining Hall.

The lower level of the McMurry Center was renovated to become the Curb Music Center and included four practice rooms and a choral room. A handsome new entrance was added along with an outdoor amphitheater. Aging Bullard Gymnasium, a landmark on campus, was reborn in 1996 with its complete renovation and rededication as the Ella Petway and George N. Bullard Center for Student Activities. Buildings were also reconfigured to fit the needs of the student body; when the Bear Lair shifted from the downstairs section of the Louise Bullard Wallace Wing to the Jack C. Massey Center for Mathematics and Science, new art spaces were formed to become the Ellis Art Studio. The dungeon of lockers that stood beneath Bullard was converted into a classroom and offices. Harpeth Hall also expanded outward in 1991 when Kirkman House was designated as the residence for the head of the school. The house had been deeded earlier to the school by the family of Patricia Kirkman Colton (W-B '48). A house on Sunnybrook Avenue was purchased which later became offices for the advancement personnel and another house on Johnstone Court was acquired.

Perhaps the most ambitious step Harpeth Hall took was in 1998 when the board approved a master plan that outlined not only future upgrades and additions but also the complete removal of traffic from the center of campus. In May 2000 the first step in carrying out the master plan occurred with the groundbreaking for the Ann Scott Carell Library. With the largest single donation in school history, the library is to be completely rebuilt with more room for the student body and state-of-the-art technology. Though Harpeth Hall has had to give up some of its acreage

Kirkman House

in return for much needed facilities, it will always retain its bucolic nature as more outdoor spaces in which students can gather to study and relax are planned, and benches and memorial trees will continue to dot the landscape.

A Change of Leadership

David Wood was headmaster during the first part of the '90s, and as Mari-Kate Hopper ('92) recalls, ". . . [he] was the quintessential Honeybear, and we all adored him." Students were guaranteed a hearty "hello" when passing him on the lawn, and his cheering and supportive face could be seen at everything from soccer games to spring dance programs. He was the type of head who, on the first cold day of winter, invited the (at the time youngest in the school) sixth graders to his Souby Hall office for hot chocolate. At Christmas to raise money for charity, he dressed as Santa and girls lined up to have their pictures taken with him. He and his wife even sponsored trips during spring break, and many students recall the educational and fun memories of those times.

LEAH RHYS

Leah Rhys assumed the position as head of school of Harpeth Hall in 1991 with a clear vision of what she wanted for the school.

"When I came, it was at a time when there had been talk about going coed and there was a fuzziness and vagueness about what the school was about," she remembers. She saw her role as one of "confirming Harpeth Hall's original mission of educating young girls and young women."

Deeply committed to single-sex education, Mrs. Rhys came to Harpeth Hall after serving seven years as head of the Laurel School in Shaker Heights, Ohio. There she worked with researchers from Harvard to create a landmark study of girls' development entitled *Meeting at the Crossroads*. "My commitment to girls' schools is how my feminism has expressed itself," she says.

Mrs. Rhys believed Harpeth Hall's core value is in developing the talents of each student. "You look for a girl's strength and provide an outlet for it," she says. During her seven years at Harpeth Hall, Mrs. Rhys provided a number of outlets, including enhancing many of the arts programs with a visiting artist and writers series and the integration of technology throughout the classes. But she feels it is the teachers who truly develop the potential in each student. "The faculty is passionate and committed to that 'ah-ha' moment for every student," she says. "Harpeth Hall truly has the best teachers I have ever seen." To support the faculty and assure even more "ah-ha" moments, three endowed faculty chairs were established for the first time during Mrs. Rhys' tenure.

Mrs. Rhys made a number of other changes to the school, including improvements in facilities for athletics and building a fitness center and amphitheater. She oversaw the addition of the fifth grade, reconstruction of Bullard Gymnasium, renovation of the Middle School lower floor and dining area and construction of the Middle School computer lab. That lab, which is housed under a cupola on the left corner of the Middle School, serves as a metaphor for how Rhys sees the school's value to the community. "If you drive by the school at night when the computer lab is lit up, it looks like a little jewel. That's how I feel Harpeth Hall is to Nashville: a tiny jewel in the middle of the city."

Nashville hasn't always seen it that way. "I felt when I first arrived that Harpeth Hall was so good but so little appreciated and ill-understood by the community," she says. "Raising its visibility was vitally important." Mrs. Rhys' efforts to make connections with the community paid off with a 25 percent increase in enrollment (back up to the 525 level of the '70s) achieved two years ahead of the schedule proposed by the board. Her efforts also resulted in an increase in the amount of financial aid, an increase in the level of annual giving from $200,000 to more than $580,000 her last year and an increase in the diversity of the school.

Involving the alumnae was also an important part of raising the school's visibility. "Understanding that the future health of the school depended on women all around the country who had benefited from their education at Harpeth Hall, I worked hard to develop contacts, traveling to cities and giving receptions for women," Mrs. Rhys says.

With her original mission complete, Mrs. Rhys retired in 1998 to Sewanee, Tennessee, where she works as a consultant for Independent Educational Services which locates heads of schools for independent schools around the country. She says her years at Harpeth Hall were "extraordinary." "I miss the excitement and the huge amount of energy of everyone there."

But, she says, she wouldn't trade. "I love this part of my life, too."

Yet during the late '80s and those early years of the '90s, Harpeth Hall, like many single-sex schools across the nation, was experiencing hard times. Harpeth Hall was at a crossroads in its history, and major changes were needed. Following Wood's resignation in 1990, Leah Rhys was selected as head of school (a title she preferred to headmistress), and in 1993 the $8.4 million capital and endowment program "Opening Doors to the Future" was launched. The school even filmed a commercial, and for years afterward, as every Harpeth Hall athlete can attest to, opposing teams would taunt the Honeybears with the chant of the now infamous line, "Harpeth Hall, we love it!" Also captured on film under Mrs. Rhys' tenure was a video documenting the heritage of Ward-Belmont and Harpeth Hall. Through the efforts of Polly Jordan

Nichols ('53), director of development, and Kitty Moon Emery ('64), president of Scene Three Productions, the video, which premiered in 1996, documented the school's past, affirmed the present and celebrated the future.

With Mrs. Rhys on board and parents and alumnae organized, the school slowly redefined its place in the world of education: it shook off its image as a place where only Nashville's wealthy sent their daughters. Mrs. Rhys aggressively sought to recruit a student body more diverse both ethnically and economically. Under her leadership, a symposium entitled "Today's Girl in Tomorrow's World" was spearheaded by Harpeth Hall in 1996 and held in conjunction with Metropolitan Nashville public schools and the Cumberland Valley Girl Scouts. It was designed according to a model by Mrs. Rhys and organized and

implemented by Hilrie Brown, director of admissions, to bring together experts—authors, psychologists, financiers, youth leaders, health professionals and many others—all of whom had a strong commitment to the education and well-being of young women. Nationally recognized professionals who were featured presenters shared their messages of expertise and encouragement to more than 1,000 attendees.

Viewpoint on Values, another initiative, came into being through a gift to bring speakers to the campus who could heighten the awareness of the importance of a value-centered community. The program also funded all-school activities designed to raise the collective level of consciousness and to weave an ethical and caring attitude into the fabric of school life. In 1999, the Harpeth Hall community chose respect, integrity, individuality and trust to be their guiding principles.

The Middle School also underwent changes in the '90s following Lindy B. Sayer's appointment as director in 1989. During her nine-year tenure, a fifth grade class was added, resulting in a true Middle School comprising fifth through

eighth grades. Faculty members began team teaching; interdisciplinary courses were taught; and science and language programs were strengthened. The Daugh W. Smith Middle School became a model, and Mrs. Sayers, whose gentle manner and friendly smile endeared her to the students, was asked to share this model with other schools throughout the southeast.

It cannot be denied that Harpeth Hall needed a push out of its comfort zone. Mrs. Rhys' legacy is one in which not only were the benefits of single-sex education renewed and the funds obtained to help ensure that there would be a Harpeth Hall for years to come, but there was also a realization of the importance of a woman's place in the world. A young girl may be told she has choices, but it is only when she understands and sees what those choices are that she may accomplish her dreams.

With some 500 girls finding their voices, however, there is bound to be conflict. At Harpeth Hall, the issues in the '90s, no matter how trivial to the outside world, were always intensely felt and hotly debated. Controversial topics ranged from responses to a cancelled Beyond Hate assembly to school uniforms to the need to consecrate the Indian remains found when the athletic facilities were expanded. From the pages of *Logos II* to the Senior House to the lunch table, students and teachers refused to shy away from conflict. In fact, it was the dialogue that was most important, for without it, Harpeth Hall would never grow or change or become the school it is today.

ANN TEAFF

In spring 2001 as alumnae, parents, faculty and friends gather to celebrate Harpeth Hall's first 50 years, Ann Teaff will be laying the groundwork for the next 50. Ms. Teaff is energized by her charge to take this exceptional school to the next level.

In her third year as head of school, the faculty is completing a year-long self-study of the school that is guided by one simple question: "Is Harpeth Hall the best it can be?"

As part of the Southern Association of Independent Schools accreditation process, Ms. Teaff is asking each faculty member to reflect on what Harpeth Hall does well and to concentrate on what it could do better. "There are a tremendous number of strengths at Harpeth Hall," she says. "We can never lose sight of that. But while we are maintaining that high standard, we must be continually improving and providing new opportunities."

The word "improve" pops up a lot when Ms. Teaff talks about the school's future. She takes the rising senior oath "to transmit this school greater, better and more beautiful than it was transmitted to us" to heart. Ms. Teaff is passionate about providing the best educational experience for the girls at Harpeth Hall. "We are studying ways to improve the math and science programs, so that even more students will be empowered by it and feel they can become doctors and engineers," she says. Three years of math is now required in the Upper School.

Ms. Teaff wants to continue to improve the use of technology throughout the school and launched the laptop initiative in the fall of 2000 that requires students in the eighth grade to own her personal laptop computer. This program will be rolled out to all grades within three years. "For technology to be useful it has to be integrated into all aspects of the classroom," says Ms. Teaff. She believes the use of the wireless technology will enhance and alter teaching styles to include fewer lectures and more group projects. These skills, she feels, will give Harpeth Hall students an advantage as they enter the workforce.

Another area Ms. Teaff wants to improve is the school's endowment. "I don't want to be solely focused on raising money, but I recognize it is an important function of this job. It is part of what we have to do to keep providing the best opportunities for the faculty and students."

While Ms. Teaff says Harpeth Hall students and faculty "are so motivated they could learn under a rock," she says continuing to upgrade facilities and providing professional development for the 73 faculty members is vital to the school's future. She remains committed to maintaining Harpeth Hall's beautiful campus and is systematically working to make sure all the school's current facilities are at their best.

Equally vital to its future is its past. Because of her pride in Harpeth Hall's rich heritage, Ms. Teaff truly values the traditions of the school. Ms. Teaff believes the school's alumnae are among its most valuable assets. She would like to see more alumnae connect with current students through events such as on-campus career panels. "It is so exciting for students to talk with alumnae who have careers they are interested in." And Ms. Teaff would like to see the alumnae network become a vital and powerful tool in supporting each other and recent Harpeth Hall graduates across the country.

Ms. Teaff, who came to Harpeth Hall after 18 years at Garrison Forest in Owings Mills, Maryland and nine years at University School of Nashville, says she hopes the alumnae returning to celebrate Harpeth Hall's birthday will feel like they are home again. "I hope they all feel a sense of belonging even if a lot of the facilities and faces have changed." She also hopes the alumnae will feel a part of the great legacy of the school and a responsibility in its future. "For Harpeth Hall to continue to improve and move forward it will require teamwork. It is an exciting time, and we have a great team."

Harpeth Hall soon found itself in the midst of another change with the departure of Mrs. Rhys and the arrival of Ann Teaff in the fall of 1998. Continuing with Mrs. Rhys' plans and with the help of the Ingram bequest, Ms. Teaff has directed the building of a wireless system for Harpeth Hall's computers. The curriculum of today is vastly different from even earlier in the '90s in that computers are an integral part of a student's education. Every teacher is outfitted with a laptop with plans for every student to be as well. On-line town meetings are held, in which issues are discussed and conferences held. Every student and teacher has an e-mail account which allows her to read the daily announcements. The use of computers is especially pertinent to the foreign language classes, for it is here that students converse and type in chat rooms, and the

teacher is later able to print out and grade their work. In the new millennium, the school introduced a laptop program which calls for all students to have a laptop computer. Ms. Teaff has also overseen the renovation of the Frances Bond Davis Theatre, the redecoration of the Marnie Sheridan Gallery and the enhancement of public areas on campus.

Overall, Ms. Teaff is a steady and calming influence on the school, her leadership strong and forthright in a world which is constantly changing. Girls are no longer content with just going to school, for they want to take an active role in their community as evidenced by the increase in volunteerism in the school. They push themselves in the traditional areas of scholarship, athletics and the arts with a greater intensity and drive than ever before.

To Be a Honeybear Is . . .

During the first assembly of the school year, Mr. Wood would stand up and say, "As the seniors go, so goes the year." They were the ones who set the tone for the year. Under their leadership the school would win championships and produce newspapers and yearbooks. Over the decade, the Senior House has been decorated with everything from camouflage to tropical scenes as each class chose colors and a hat to represent them. Most of those seniors came to the school years before when they were several inches smaller, years younger and a little more than unsure how this "all girls thing" would work out. In the end, though, they graduate knowing they have spent their formative years in an environment where academics, traditions and friendships are all equally valued.

During her time at Harpeth Hall, a student more than likely sold grapefruit for her sophomore class's fund raiser, gladly paid a dollar to wear jeans and a sweater on any number of "Duds Days" and agonized over whether to choose Barb and Judes' tea cakes or peanut butter cookies for dessert at lunch. She may have held a position on the Honor Council or traveled on the school's Winterim trip to Greece and Egypt. In eighth grade, she probably spent hours in Mrs. Mabry's office, laughing and killing time while ignoring the Middle School administrative assistant's cries to "Let me get some work done around here." As a 15-year-old worried about having to finish

Winterim 1999

chemistry problems and a term paper in one night, she may have had what is commonly referred to as an emotional breakdown. Her friends, however, would comfort her, but then casually step over her prostrate body in order to arrive to

their own classes on time, for they know the routine—they already had one themselves earlier in the week.

Every class at Harpeth Hall is different; like a family, each girl plays a role, and when graduation day arrives, the quirks and eccentricities, the traits that over the years have inspired, encouraged and even annoyed are celebrated as having contributed to the achievements of the class. Because day in and day out the class struggled and succeeded together, there is a bond that will forever be there. Friendships are formed for life, and those moments when one aced an algebra test, ate lunch on the senior patio or gave a speech in assembly will form the backdrop of experience that an individual carries with her forever.

A History of Professionals

The sense of community and closeness that permeates Harpeth Hall is in large part due to the faculty and administration. Scores of alumnae maintain that their teachers at Harpeth Hall far overshadow any they may have had in college or beyond. Varina Buntin ('95) describes the faculty as "devoting themselves to their students with patience and brilliance, enthusiasm and originality, support and more support . . . These people taught me to think. To think and care about that thinking, to feel proud of it, always to do it as a ward against ignorance and complacency." Lauren Marler ('94)

recalls former physics teacher Dr. Heath Jones and the care which he took to record his lectures for her the year she took two weeks off to study in France. Many times as she sat at her kitchen counter listening to each 50-minute tape, a family member would walk through and invariably pause to laugh or marvel at the way in which Dr. Jones brought a subject as strenuous as physics to life.

The sense of community is heightened by the fact that many of the teachers have been at Harpeth Hall for many years. The shared experiences of one generation of students can be carried on into the next because of continuity, an assurance that when one comes back to visit, there will be someone there who knows her, who saw her grow up. To this day, many girls who have passed through the school still cannot chew gum in public for fear of encountering retired physical education teacher

Pat Neblett Moran's (W-B '51) strict vigilance and piercing whistle. Under former biology teacher Carolyn Felkel dozens of girls were crowned "Frog Queen" for their excellent work in the dissection of that year's amphibians. A potter, she fashioned necklaces for the recipients of various awards to wear with the whole ceremony which culminated in a procession and burial down by the tennis courts. There is Dr. Jack Henderson and his guitar, Joyce Crutcher Ward ('60) and her undying enthusiasm for the classics and Marian Ross, the accompanist without whom no concert or play would be complete.

And then there is the "male posse," a name students years ago gave to that long-standing group of Upper School male teachers who bravely surround themselves with emotional teenagers every day. Legendary European history teacher and founding member Dr. Art Echerd says it is those moments when you find former students returning that you understand why you teach and the difference you can make in another's life. "You realize that, if you had not been teaching back when she was in high school, you would never have had the opportunity to know such an exceptional person. When that occurs, it makes you aware of how rewarding your job can be, but it also reminds you that someday you will almost certainly be feeling the same way about some of the students you are currently teaching. This is one of the reasons why I try to attend as many Harpeth Hall events as I can. The longer you teach at a place, the more conscious you are of how quickly students pass through the school. They are gone before you know it, so, whenever possible, you need to try to attend their plays, their concerts, their sporting events, their academic competitions, or whatever, because soon the opportunity to do so will be gone forever." Perhaps this is why the graduates of Harpeth Hall feel that their time there was so special; the faculty and the administration are devoted not only to instilling knowledge into their students but also to ensuring that they are supported, cared for and loved as the spectacular women they will most assuredly become.

MEMORIES

"Tuzeneu was not afraid to jump from his windowsill wearing a Harley Davidson helmet, chanting French verb conjugations to make us remember them. Margaret Renkl took us on walks through the woods to define 'poetry' for us, and she sold me on Shakespeare. Dr. Myers felt passionately about every slide she flashed before us, and her passion was contagious. Diann Blakely (Shoaf) introduced us into her class stating she expected us to feel as if we were drowning. She then said she would not come rescue us but would stand on the shore and cheer."   —Varina Buntin ('95)

"Through Mr. Goodwin's class I acquired a love for the art of photography, but more importantly, I learned that not many things in the world are just black and white. The ability to recognize the beauty of a situation from different perspectives and angles allows one to truly appreciate the shades of gray that constantly surround us."
—Katie Moran ('94)

"Dr. Myers taught me more than any teacher I have ever encountered. Her interest in her students combined with her ability to connect present-day reality with art and literature provide her with an extraordinary gift that every student should have the opportunity to enjoy. I think of her daily."
—Comer Ireland ('96)

Traditions of the Past, Traditions of the Future

Harpeth Hall is founded on the traditions of the past, and over the years those traditions have both stayed the same yet at the same time evolved to fit the burgeoning needs of the student body. For years, the pages in the Lady of the Hall's court wore outfits that can only be described as "elflike." In the early '90s, it was decided that a simple white dress would be not only more practical but comfortable as well. The club system has also changed; every year girls are still divided into

the four groups, but instead of initiation rites filled with seventh graders in face paint, dyed hair, and various gator, eagle, ladybug and whale outfits, there are now intramurals, song and quiz bowl competitions. The seniors still participate in a Renaissance Banquet, and the student council still sponsors talent shows and a welcome back-to-school Concert on the Lawn. Of course, standards such as the seventh grade's George Washington Birthday Celebration continue to take place, for the year wouldn't be complete if the whole school didn't turn out at 8:00 A.M. to witness the Revolutionary Army's hurried steps or the sailor's "broken ankle" dance.

At Harpeth Hall, though many of the traditions may be old, new ones are constantly being created. In the Middle School and beginning with the eighth grade class of '91, a Halloween Carnival was started for the children of alumnae, and every year it has grown in scope and size so that now it is a standing rite each fall. In the Upper School, the annual Community Day has been transformed into a whole year of ongoing volunteer opportunities. Instead of the entire school disbanding for a single day of goodwill, girls can now choose, with the help of a volunteer coordinator and the Key Club, from a plethora of events in which the greater Nashville area will benefit. Over the years, Habitat for Humanity houses have been built and debris from tornado damage has been cleared by Harpeth Hall volunteers.

PROM THEMES
Escape to Egypt
Paradise Lost
Neptune's Night Out
An Evening with the Stars
Arabian Nights
Mardi Gras: A Night in New Orleans
Escape to Vegas
Shipwrecked on Treasure Island
Welcome to Hollywood
Enchanted Evening
No Place Like Prom: Welcome to Emerald City

In the *Milestones* yearbook one can still find the language clubs, the drama's Playmakers and Mock Trial, but as the years go by more and more organizations fill its pages. The 1990s saw the addition of an outdoor education coordinator and a program that allows for day hikes and overnight camping trips. Beyond Hate pushed the Harpeth Hall community to educate itself on matters of racism and prejudice, while the Student Ambassadors promoted the attributes of the school with tours and phon-a-thons. Because Harpeth Hall cheerleaders became nonexistent in the '90s, the pep club was even more vital. On the days when a particular sport had a big game and was therefore in

need of major support, it arranged for the various Pack the Pool, Jam the Gym and Flood the Field activities. When the basketball team made it to the state final four for the first time in history, it was the pep club that organized the rag-tag band of cheerleaders on the sidelines. Clad in an assortment of old uniforms, tube socks and tennis shoes, the girls made such an impression on the city of Murfreesboro and the officials of the tournament that when it came time to hand out the spirit awards, Harpeth Hall not only won for its division but secured a place on the front page of the daily paper.

These people taught me to think . . . and care about that thinking, to feel proud of it, always to do it as a ward against ignorance and complacency.
—Lauren Marler ('94)

A New Generation of Women's Athletics

At Harpeth Hall, the cheer "The will to win can not be beat, you got to want to win. Go Harpeth Hall," was yelled before every competition. In the summer, when there was 100 percent humidity, the soccer team was out on the field scrimmaging,

and, in the early spring, when the air was cold and the sky was letting loose with a rainstorm, the track team was running laps for an interval workout. On their own in the off-season, girls shot free throws in a lonely gym or practiced their serve out on the tennis court. In the end, these girls have learned how to be leaders, how to sacrifice for the team and, most importantly, how to succeed through victories and through failures.

During the '90s, Harpeth Hall had eight state championship teams, 32 regional championship teams, and numerous recipients of all-state, all-region and all-metro honors. At Harpeth Hall, where academics come first, sports have steadily grown in importance and participation. It wasn't until the late '70s and early '80s that Harpeth Hall even engaged in competition with other schools, for until that time intramurals were the only sports available. With the advent of Title IX, colleges across the country increased and developed their women's athletic programs, with the result being that more and more high school teams were established. In the late '80s, the swimming and diving team was composed of only a few dedicated girls who drove to Pearl Cohn for

practices, while in the '99-'00 school year, 29 girls were on the roster, and several were selected for All-American status.

The will to win can not be beat, you got to want to win. Go Harpeth Hall!

FEMALE ATHLETES

It is this generation of female athletes, a group that has never known a time when sports were not available to them, a group that has never had to sit by and simply watch the boys play who are competing today. They assume they can play in college and even professionally. Susan Russ, director of athletics and head cross-country and track coach, says, "It has been a gradual process . . . but the excellence in academics has carried over into athletics."

Katherine Wray ('95), a three-sport veteran, says that "athletics were an extremely important part of my Harpeth Hall experience and really helped to shape the person that I am today. Playing volleyball and tennis for Mrs. Moran and basketball for Mr. Springman, my teammates and I experienced a full range of emotions, from the utter joy of victory to the bitter disappointment of defeat to love and concern for each other."

Though there are students at Harpeth Hall who do go on to participate in college athletics, most do not, choosing instead to take their memories and lessons learned as athletes out into the greater world. For Katherine Wray ('95) it was the sheer joy of team victory. She says, "I remember when our basketball team was playing Coach Springman's alma mater in St. Louis, and the game came down to the wire. We decided to run a play that was named after the school we were playing, Marquette, and we executed it perfectly, with Mary Southwood ('94) laying the ball in just as the buzzer sounded. We were so excited you'd have thought we'd won the NCAA's!" For others, it is every time Mrs. Russ gathered together her team in a circle, pinkies linked, for one of her signature inspirational talks. For most, however, it is those simple moments when a friend and teammate displays profound courage and commitment. Such is the case of Kate Terry ('94) who in the spring of her senior year qualified for the state track meet in the 400 meters, after having spent the previous year out with cancer. With coaches, teachers and schoolmates surrounding the field cheering her on, she ran a race that can never be rivaled in terms of true heart and determination. As Mrs. Russ so aptly phrased it, "If there is going to be athletics for girls, then Harpeth Hall is going to do it and do it well."

Singers, Actors, Painters, Dancers

The arts have long held a position of importance within the curriculum at Harpeth Hall, and the opportunities for students to express themselves and showcase their talents has grown. With the renovation of the art studio, students in the '90s had more room in which to develop their talents under the watchful eye of art teachers Ann Blackburn, Rosie Paschall and Cati Vietorisz. During the school year students may take trips out of town to see exhibits or display their work in the Upper School art exhibit. Almost every year there have also been several medalists in the Cheekwood art competition. Many alumnae and professional artists such as Susie Creagh ('90) and Stephanie Paddock Cook ('93) first began to explore their chosen careers while still at Harpeth Hall.

Theatre at Harpeth Hall grew exponentially in the '90s, thanks in part to the leadership of Janette Fox Klocko, theatre director. Where before there was simply a fall musical and a spring drama, Shakespeare and student-directed one-acts became standard, too. Often the whole school turned out to see the sell-out performances such as the joint production between MBA and Harpeth Hall of the musical *Grease*. With teachers even stepping in to fill roles, the dramas put on by the cast and crew known as Playmakers were highly professional and expertly executed feats of theatrical arts.

The music program also expanded with the creation of a combined Montgomery Bell Academy and Harpeth Hall orchestra. In the '90s, the program grew to two Middle School choruses, an Upper School chorus that performed throughout the community and assorted small chamber music ensembles. Instead of the occasional violin player treating the school to a teaser of her abilities, students were encouraged to contribute their talents to the growing musical community. As a result, everything from the harp to the flute could be heard during school productions.

In the eyes of Leslie Matthews, one of her greatest memories was seeing the dance program progress over the 23 years she has been at Harpeth Hall. At the close of the decade, she returned to full-time teaching in the curriculum, passing the responsibility of the dance company to former student, Tina Trinkler Cowlyn ('83). More than 60 girls participated

in the dance company with many more taking dance as a course during the school day. During Winterim, trips were often taken to such places as New York, where the girls took classes and saw professional dance companies perform.

In the '90s, Harpeth Hall initiated and instituted various programs for the whole school. Assemblies featured the Carell Visiting Artist and Writer Series. Every year during Awards Day the accomplishments of not only scholars but also artists were recognized. With the Cindy Crist Art Purchase Award, a student's work was bought and hung within the school. Works of the recipients of the Kirkman House Art Award are on display in the house. The written word was also celebrated with the publication of Harpeth Hall's literary magazine, *Hallmarks*, whose staff one year compiled a compact disc of their songs and poems. Each year interest in the arts at Harpeth Hall has grown stronger.

While many facets of Harpeth Hall changed vastly in the 1990s, the school with its great magnolias, white brick buildings, green lawns and daffodils remained, as Varina Buntin ('95) writes, ". . . a feeling, a place, a community—that you have to know and in knowing come to love." It is that time in a young girl's life where friendships form as thick as blood, and mentors are found who influence students in ways only revealed years later.

SCHOOL PRODUCTIONS MIDDLE SCHOOL

Babes in Toyland
Hundred Acre Wood in Pooh Forest
Alice in Wonderland
The Velveteen Rabbit
Kiddleywinks
I Believe in Make Believe
Schoolhouse Rocks
Conestoga Stories
Don't Count Your Chickens
    Before They Cry Wolf

SCHOOL MUSICALS UPPER SCHOOL

No, No Nanette
Godspell
Anything Goes
Pippin
Cinderella
Oklahoma!
Guys and Dolls
Grease

The Future of Harpeth Hall

In another 50 years, as Harpeth Hall celebrates its first centennial, we can predict with assurance that the leaders of the school will have as rich and successful a story to tell as the one in this book. The foundation of providing a quality education for young women which was so firmly established through Ward Seminary, Belmont College and Ward-Belmont is still seen today in the classroom, assembly and in each girl's bright future. Harpeth Hall will continue to build upon that foundation in the years to come.

PRESIDENTIAL SCHOLARS

The first Harpeth Hall student to be named a Presidential Scholar was Brooke Graham ('90). Presidential Scholars are selected among students nationwide for their demonstrated scholarship, leadership, contribution to the school and community and exceptional accomplishments. Later in the decade, Lola Blackwell ('97) and Kristina Treanor ('98) were honored as Presidential Scholars. Kristina Treanor invited Carol Oxley, her most influential teacher, to attend the White House-sponsored ceremony with her. Mrs. Oxley, a member of Harpeth Hall's faculty for 29 years, had been Kristina's math teacher for two years and was honored with a Certificate of Excellence.

In the meantime, there are some near-term goals that reflect the collective vision for the school in its next 10 years. Obviously, the key focus for the board of trust in the next five years will be raising $35 million to implement the remaining objectives outlined in the 1998 strategic plan. While this is an ambitious campaign with a goal more than four times as much as has been raised in past capital and endowment efforts, both administrators and board members are enthusiastic and confident of success. A successful campaign will mean a substantial increase in the endowment that today stands just over $10 million.

Additionally, campus expansion and improvement designed to strengthen the educational program include a new state-of-the-art library, enlarged and renovated Upper and Middle Schools and a central core of the campus that is more student-friendly. Roads and parking will be concentrated on the periphery for safety and to maximize use of available space.

The most important responsibility of the board of trust is to ensure that the mission of the school is fulfilled. In short, that means that a superior academic program conducive to equipping and motivating each student to meet her greatest potential must be in place. There is no more critical aspect in reaching

this goal than attracting and retaining the highest caliber faculty. Harpeth Hall's faculty has always been superlative, and the vision for the future is to continue to build on that tradition. A primary focus will be to continue to increase salaries, benefits and professional development funds coupled with assuring that the learning environment is second to none. Expanded spaces for science, athletics and fitness, and faculty offices are part of the longer-term dream for the school.

Furthermore, Harpeth Hall will continue to serve as an educational resource for the broader Nashville community and the nation. Recognized as one of the foremost educational institutions for girls, the school in a sense serves as a laboratory for studying how girls learn best and has a responsibility to share best practices. Faculty members are called on regularly to speak across the nation to teachers desiring to imitate various aspects of the Harpeth Hall experience. The school is praised today as an excellent model of integrating technology into the classroom. With laptops scheduled for all students within three years and a finished library with the latest technological capabilities, there is no doubt that Harpeth Hall's program will continue to be cited as cutting edge.

It takes an army of committed people focused on a common goal to make good things happen. Harpeth Hall is blessed by strong leadership in Ann Teaff as head of school, highly engaged and talented faculty and hard-working alumnae, parents and trustees. Their common goal is simple: to see Harpeth Hall become the finest single-gender educational institution for girls in the nation. And if the past is any reflection of what might happen in the future, there is no doubt that goal will be realized.

THE SPIRIT OF HARPETH HALL

The buildings and the faces change from year to year, but students all are woven into the same fabric that is Harpeth Hall. As the seats fold up after assembly, the energetic voices proclaiming, "Hooray for Freshman" continue to blend with the more experienced refrain "Are You a Senior?"

Hooray for Freshman, Hooray for Freshman,
Someone in the crowd yell hooray for Freshman,
Two, four, six, eight who do we appreciate?
Freshmen that's who!

Are you a Senior?
Yes I'm a Senior!
S-E-N-I-O-R Seniors are the Best!
Are you a Senior?
Yes I'm a Senior!
'Cause Seniors are the Best!

BEHIND THE SCENES

The alumnae association, the board of trust and the parents association presently form the support system for Harpeth Hall. The board of trust has existed since the school's inception, with the responsibilities of initiating and developing the business aspects of the school, as well as gathering resources to assure an environment in which students and faculty may thrive.

The need for the associations, however, was only perceived in the 1960s. When Idanelle McMurry became headmistress in 1963, she quickly realized that alumnae information was lacking for Ward-Belmont and Harpeth Hall. She began the process of recovering the information and encouraging the formation of the alumnae association.

The first recorded evidence of a parents association also came in 1963, during Miss

McMurry's tenure. Over the years, parents have become increasingly involved in Harpeth Hall activities and have played an integral role in the school's growth and development.

Alumnae Association

In 1963 Idanelle McMurry asked Linda Williams Dale ('56) to form an alumnae association and begin the process of recovering all the Ward-Belmont and Harpeth Hall alumnae information. Miss McMurry wanted to be able to communicate with alumnae through a newsletter and keep alumnae in touch with the school. The alumnae association charter was drawn up, and in 1964, the constitution was adopted with Linda Williams Dale as the first president. She served for an amazing term of 10 years.

In 1969 upon Linda's request, the first officers to serve with her were Dede Bullard Wallace ('53) as vice president, Sally Jordan Minnigan ('52) as treasurer, Elinor Berger Peek ('60) as recording secretary and Linda Christie Moynihan ('57) as historian. The purpose of the alumnae association was two-fold: to be a means of continuing friendships and to foster a continued personal and financial commitment to the school. The alumnae association met twice each year. It encouraged alumnae to return to campus; to meet Sam McMurry and to see firsthand the huge needs on campus; and to act as goodwill ambassadors and solicitors. Jeanne Pilkerton Zerfoss (W-B '43) joined in the effort to update the class lists from Ward-Belmont and Harpeth Hall before creating the the first alumnae newsletter in 1971. In 1973, based on Jeanne Pilkerton Zerfoss's recommendation, Polly Jordan Nichols ('53) was hired to be the first paid director of alumnae.

In 1975 alumnae records were sufficiently complete to establish the Alumnae Annual Giving Program. Prior to this time, alumnae paid annual dues. Subsequently, Ward-Belmont alumnae records were brought up-to-date, and Harpeth Hall issued a Ward-Belmont directory.

In 1990, the bylaws of the alumnae association were amended to reflect the future direction of the association. The position of president changed from a two-year term to a one-year term, and the position of president-elect was added to allow a year of experience prior to assuming the role of president. The alumnae giving chair position was also added. Working in conjunction with the development office, this individual coordinated the alumnae aspect of annual giving.

POLLY JORDAN NICHOLS ('53)

Polly Jordan Nichols has carried the story of Harpeth Hall within her for more than half of her life. As a sophomore at Ward-Belmont in the spring of 1951, Polly was one of the faithful who, along with her family, supported the founding of The Harpeth Hall School after the unexpected closure of Ward-Belmont in that year. She now likes to say, "I had the best of both worlds—two years at each school." She was the Salutatorian of her class, and she also won the Citizenship Bracelet, an award that continues to be meaningful to Ms. Nichols. She has always known that Harpeth Hall prepared its students extremely well for higher education as evidenced by her acceptance and success at Radcliffe College in the 1950s.

Just as the founding families believed in a need for the continuation of a fine girl's school in Nashville, one that was based on relationships, trust and commitment, so has Ms. Nichols continued her devotion to Harpeth Hall. After 13 years away from Nashville, she moved back and began volunteering at Harpeth Hall in 1971. Two years later, she accepted the first official alumnae director position, a part-time job. It would be through her tireless work and learning through experience that prompted Headmaster David Wood to ask Ms. Nichols to work full-time as the school's first director of development. She has worked with four of the five heads of school and was a student under the first. She has worked with nine of the ten board of trustees presidents, beginning with board chair, Daugh W. Smith, one of the school's five founders. In doing so, Ms. Nichols can be credited with the success of the school's advancement programs. She has helped guide almost every major building campaign, and initiated and expanded the Annual Giving, Capital and Endowment, and Planned Giving Programs.

Ms. Nichols received the Dede Bullard Wallace Award at commencement in 1986 for outstanding service to the school, and at her retirement in January 2000 after 27 years of service, it was announced that the proposed History Wall would be dedicated in her name.

Sarah Nichols, ('83), Polly Nichols ('53), Britton Nielsen, Trustee

In 1999, Emily Perkins Zerfoss ('75) president of the alumnae association, and Sarah W. Nichols ('83), president-elect, were asked to serve as the chairs of Harpeth Hall's 50th anniversary to be held in the year 2000-2001. The activities planned included the publication of this book, a Ward-Belmont reunion, an alumnae holiday reception, an alumnae art exhibit and an elaborate Gala Celebration in May 2001. In addition, students and parents planned events on campus, including a Women of Distinction speakers series, a Founders Day celebration and a time capsule. [*Editor's Note:* a special thanks to Mrs. Zerfoss and Miss Nichols for their persistence and dedication in the publication of this book.]

As always, alumnae support for Harpeth Hall remains strong. Harpeth Hall's more than 3,000 alumnae are devoted to the school and appreciative of the value system, high academic standards and the excellent liberal arts education that serves each alumna for a lifetime and the friendships that last just as long.

Alumnae Activities

From chairing capital campaigns to manning phones during the annual phon-a-thon, alumnae have played an active role in fund raising for Harpeth Hall. The "Hang-Up" (resale of uniforms), now run by the parents association, was initiated by alumnae. The Annual Giving Program is led by alumnae who fill positions including alumnae gift chair, reunion general chair, major gifts chair and class fund raising chair.

Over the years there have been many varied gatherings for the alumnae and their families. In 1978, alumnae under the leadership of Carolyn Russell ('64) organized the first Alumnae Art Exhibit, which took place in the Marnie Sheridan Art Gallery. In 1979, an Alumnae Night featured Fred Russell, Carolyn's father and the *Tennessean's* sports writer, as guest speaker and paid tribute to Miss McMurry prior to her departure.

Run for the Green 1987

In 1987, the Run for the Green fun-run was held on the new track at Harpeth Hall for all alumnae. In addition, alumnae have been invited back to campus for dances, plays, programs and receptions of all kinds throughout the years.

Other get-togethers, such as the annual Easter Egg Hunt and Halloween Carnival, include the children of alumnae. The alumnae association has also hosted the Mother-Daughter Tea and a holiday reception.

Alumnae receptions held in other cities have been ongoing, but under the leadership of Head of School Leah Rhys, at least two out-of-town receptions took place each year. Receptions have been held in New York City, Washington, D.C., Boston, Chicago, San Francisco, Atlanta, Dallas, Houston and cities throughout Tennessee.

Alumnae Halloween Party 1998

In 1997, a continuing education program was initiated by the alumnae association. The purpose of the program is to further the education of the alumnae, address an identified need and bring more alumnae back to campus both as recognized experts and as students. Sarah W. Nichols ('83) was the first alumnae association officer to head up this effort. In the fall of 1997 the nine highly diverse course offerings included Internet training, a Spanish refresher, investment strategies and a wine-tasting. In October 1999, the first golf tournament, The Souby, was held, with alumnae, students, parents and faculty in attendance. Amy Grant ('78) served as honorary chair.

By virtue of the website www.harpethhall.com, developed in the spring of 1997, alumnae now have a way to learn about current activities of the association, sign up for events, update their records with the school and stay connected with alumnae and the school.

Continuing Education 1997

Alumnae Holiday Reception 1997

In honor of the class of 1975's reunion held in May 2000, alumnae Vanessa Draper and Betsy Koonce Sottek penned and performed this song during reunion weekend and produced a commemorative compact disc. Classmate Celia "Ducky" Gulbenk accompanied on keyboards.

We had the promised land before us
And the blessing of a well worn path
We never hesitated, never thought to stop
Never did look back
And they taught the children well
To believe in themselves
And now we're standing here
Ever thankful for the years.

It's been a quarter of a century
Since we stepped away
And stepped out on our own
We've lived a lifetime between then and now
But it's always easy to come home.

And the years fell away
Like the leaves in the fall
Changin' seasons
But never changing much at all.

We often wonder where those girls in plaid have gone
Looking back—it's more than memories
It is a legacy of liberty
The freedom to be all that we can be.

And they taught the children well
To believe in themselves
And now we're standing here
Ever thankful for the years.

Reunions

The first reunion of Ward-Belmont alumnae after Harpeth Hall was formed was held in March 1968 with almost 900 graduates from 37 states attending [*See* Chapter 1]. The second Ward-Belmont reunion was held in 1986 and attended by 600 graduates. In October 2000, more than 300 "belles" participated in the most recent reunion. Beginning in the 1990s, Ward-Belmont and Harpeth Hall class reunions were combined and held together on the same weekend in May.

Throughout the years, there have been many reunions of Harpeth Hall alumnae. In 1980, a First Four Classes reunion was held which included the graduates of the classes of 1952, 1953, 1954 and 1955. In the 1970s and 1980s, many classes tended to have a reunion every five to ten years and featured dinners at classmates' homes and picnics with alumnae and their children. In 1976, all alumnae were invited to attend a reunion to celebrate Harpeth Hall's 25th anniversary, organized by Alva Herbert Wilk ('59), alumnae association president, and reunion chair Carolyn Russell ('64). Held on campus on June 4, 1976, the celebration included a tennis tournament, a bridge tournament, tours of the school, a picnic lunch, and alumnae and teacher skits. The founders of the school were also honored.

Under the direction of Ingelein Smith Walker ('78) in the fall of 1988, Harpeth Hall started organizing reunions for classes in

Grand Reunion Luncheon 1998

five year intervals. In 1989, Dianne Buttrey Wild ('66) assumed this role from Ms. Walker and actually oversaw the first set of reunions held in this manner. In 1997, Sallie King Norton ('71) became director of alumnae relations when Dianne Buttrey Wild ('66) became Harpeth Hall's director of admissions.

In 1993, during the tenure of Leah Rhys and under the leadership of Mrs. Wild as associate director of alumnae and development and Ms. Nichols as director of development, reunions were greatly expanded to include the goals called the 3 R's: reunite with classmates, reconnect to the school and reconsider personal giving to the school. Reunions are designated as the first weekend in May. Each class has a reunion chair(s) that serve on the reunion steering committee, act as fund raising chairs and staff the reunion phon-a-thons. Reunion giving has comprised the largest part of alumnae giving to the annual fund, exceeding $100,000 for the first time in the reunion year 2000.

Grand Reunion Luncheon 1999

Reunion weekend includes a wine and cheese faculty/alumnae reception for all reunion classes at Kirkman House, a breakfast for the oldest reunion class, a panel discussion featuring knowledgeable alumnae and the Grand Reunion Luncheon. The weekend also features events planned by individual classes, such as a girls' night out, a cocktail party with spouses and picnics for the entire family.

In 1996, the first Almost Alumnae Luncheon for seniors was initiated. Held in May prior to reunion weekend, it is a celebration of their impending graduation and inclusion in the alumnae association.

Distinguished Alumna Award

The Harpeth Hall/Ward-Belmont Distinguished Alumna Award was established in 1993. During Leah Rhys' tenure and under the direction of committee chairman Lissa Luton Bradford ('55), the original selection committee was responsible for determining the criteria for the award and establishing the process by which the recipient would be chosen, as well as selecting the first distinguished alumna recipient. The criteria they established are that the candidates are trailblazers; display extraordinary gifts of leadership and organizational ability; are moving spirits in health, welfare, cultural or civic affairs; have achieved wide recognition for professional excellence and leadership, serving as an example for other women; have attained unusual success in highly competitive fields; and/or are nationally recognized for vision, skill and commitment to make things happen.

Each year a committee of both local and out-of-town alumnae representing different decades is charged with the task of reviewing the nominations, which are submitted by alumnae, and making the selection of the award recipient. Presented annually at the Grand Reunion Luncheon, Distinguished Alumna Awards to date have been presented to:

1993   Sarah Ophelia Colley Cannon (W-B '32). Nationally recognized for service to mankind. As Minnie Pearl, internationally recognized as a performing artist.

1994   Florence Wates Pert (W-B '49). Senior Associate Minister, Marble Collegiate Church, New York. First woman to be ordained in the 360-year history of the church.

1995   Dr. Mildred Stahlman (W-B '40). Began the first newborn intensive care unit in the country to use respiratory therapy on newborns with damaged lungs. Professor of Pediatrics and Pathology at Vanderbilt University Medical School.

1995   Ann Stahlman Hill (W-B '39). Devoted to the arts. Served on the board of the Nashville Academy Theater for 50 years and is a Fellow of the American Theater.

1996   Amy Grant ('78). World-renowned singer and songwriter. Exceptional community volunteer. In 1994 received the prestigious Pax Christian Award by the Benedictine Order at St. John's University, one of only three women to have done so.

1997   Nancy Rule Goldberger ('52). Widely recognized for her research on topics of women's development and cultural diversity, adolescent and student development, innovative student-centered education and ways of knowing.

1998   Marguerite Weaver Sallee ('64). Trailblazing business leader who made extraordinary accomplishments in family and children's issues. Presently Chairman and CEO of Frontline Group, which offers corporate training services and President and CEO of Corporate Family Solutions, now known as Bright Horizons Family Solutions, which she helped co-found in 1987. She was the first woman to be named chairman of the Nashville Area Chamber of Commerce.

1999   Idanelle McMurry (W-B '43). Pioneer in women's education. Headmistress of Harpeth Hall from 1963-1979.

2000   Tracy Caulkins Stockwell ('81). Internationally recognized athlete. Olympic swimmer, winning three gold medals in the 1984 Olympics.

DISTINGUISHED ALUMNAE

Sarah Ophelia Cannon
1993

Florence Wates Pert
1994

Dr. Mildred Stahlman
1995

Ann Stahlman Hill
1995

Amy Grant
1996

Nancy Rule Goldberger
1997

Marguerite Weaver Sallee
1998

Idanelle McMurry
1999

Tracy Caulkins Stockwell
2000

Board of Trustees

Each of the 10 board of trust chairs has exemplified visionary leadership for Harpeth Hall. From the 25 years of service by Dr. Daugh W. Smith (21 years as board chair) to the normal two-year term served by most chairs, each one has initiated positive changes while promoting preservation of essential traditions. Dr. Smith and Ellen Bowers Hofstead (W-B '34) have been honored with the distinction of life member emeritus upon retirement from the board.

To understand the ongoing activity at the school, each board member is encouraged to schedule time for classroom visits during the fall to obtain an appreciation for the daily work of the faculty and students and to gain empirical information regarding their needs and accomplishments.

To initiate actions decided by the board, the committees meet on a regular basis primarily on the campus. The executive committee meets monthly to conduct business between board meetings. The standing committees consist of finance, development, long-range planning and nomination. The president appoints committee members, who are not required to be board members, with approval by the board. Additional integral committees include buildings and grounds, diversity, education, student life, planned gifts and trustee ambassadors.

The success of major fund-raising campaigns to increase the campus facility and provide financial security for operations has been achieved through tireless efforts of board members such as Jeanne Pilkerton Zerfoss (W-B '43) for the $1 million endowment fund campaign in 1972; Barbara Massey Rogers ('56) and Ed Nelson for the 1975-1978 McMurry Center campaign; Britton H. Nielsen and Mary Schlater Stumb ('53) for the $3 million capital campaign of 1983-86; Norris Nielsen for the 1987 athletic complex fund raising; and Don Johnston, Ken Melkus and Dr. Robert West for the $8.4 million capital and endowment campaign of 1993-98. The combined efforts of the latter three men for the more recently formed leadership giving concept of the capital and endowment program proved a positive force for increased annual contributions to the school.

Other significant contributors to the fund-raising efforts have been Lulu Hampton Owen, Patricia Frist and Martha Ingram. Norris Nielsen, Luke Simons and Eugene Pargh were instrumental in forming wise investment plans for endowed

funds. As recent chair of the finance committee, Derril Reeves educated the board on being good stewards of the funds entrusted.

Successful searches were chaired by Sue Ivie for Idanelle McMurry (W-B '43); Jeanne Pilkerton Zerfoss (W-B '43) for David Wood; Carol Clark Elam ('66) for Leah Rhys; and Varina Frazer Buntin ('61) for Ann Teaff. Heading the nominating committee to find new trustees was one of the many accomplishments of Jackie Glover Thompson ('64), who served on the board for more than 17 years. Ten years in the making, the search for methods to bring Harpeth Hall into the technology forefront was due to concentrated efforts of Rick Oliver as board chair in 1990 and Paula Hughey ('66). John Morris, Martha Ingram and Paula Hughey supplied resources for funding technological updates to the campus.

In the area of long-range planning, Mary Schlater Stumb ('53), Jack Jacques and Anne Davis ('73) have provided strong leadership. Mary Stumb has held almost every volunteer position and has been instrumental in the success of the planned giving program. To retain faculty and provide competitive benefits that would place Harpeth Hall in the top 10 percent of the region, Peggy Smith Warner ('54) as board chair helped to implement Leah Rhys' vision. Retaining the involvement of the Ward-Belmont alumnae has been the ongoing responsibility and achievement of Emmie Jackson McDonald (W-B '44). The increasingly beautiful grounds and buildings have been enhanced by members such as Patricia Kirkman Colton (W-B '48) [Kirkman House], John Rochford, Rick Scott and Tara Crenshaw Armistead ('75).

National Advisory Council

Conceived by the board of trustees in 1997, the national advisory council serves to promote the general welfare of Harpeth Hall. The council strives to become familiar with the mission of Harpeth Hall and its implementation in all areas; to work with and give counsel to the board and the head of the school; to participate in an ongoing evaluation of the long-range plans for the school; to assist in developing Harpeth Hall through support for present and future programs for the school; and to host events to bring together influential and representative alumnae and individuals who will serve as informed and enthusiastic ambassadors for Harpeth Hall in their communities.

FIRST NATIONAL ADVISORY COUNCIL MEMBERS

Linda Blair Cline ('68)	Chicago, IL
Louise Bilbro Connell ('66)	New Canaan, CT
Carol Clark Elam ('66)	Nashville, TN
Cey Gray ('83)	San Francisco/ New York
Paula Hughey ('66)	Atlanta, GA
Christine Johnston Johnson ('89)	Boston, MA
Lisa Morrissey LaVange ('71)	Chapel Hill, NC
Jean Nelson ('65), Chair	Nashville, TN
Florence Wates Pert (W-B '49)	New York, NY
Marguerite Weaver Sallee ('64)	Nashville, TN
Tracy Caulkins Stockwell ('81)	Queensland, Australia
Ellen Bronaugh Vergos ('68)	Memphis, TN
Lucy Van Voorhees ('67)	Washington, DC
Emily Perkins Zerfoss ('75)	Nashville, TN

In the fall of 1999, the council organized Harpeth Hall's Career Day, which consisted of a panel discussion for grades 7-12 featuring five professional alumnae and lunch discussion groups for juniors and seniors with advisory council members. In addition, the advisory council organized monthly lunch meetings between alumnae and students. The advisory council's future plans include on-line communication between alumnae and students to establish career networks. Carol Clark Elam ('66), board of trustees president (1998-2000), stated that a primary task of the council is to help the school develop a career mentoring program.

Please join us for a Career Day Assembly honoring 40 years of women's education at The Harpeth Hall School on February 11, 1991 at 8:00 a.m.
Davis Auditorium
Speakers:
Tish Fort Schermerhorn '56
interior designer

Ginger Osborn Justus '66
Assistant Professor of Philosophy
Belmont College

Libby Oldfield Broadhurst, M.D. '73
OB/GYN

Kelley Sanders '85 NASA
research assoc/mgr microgravity support

Libby Oldfield Broadhurst ('73)

Parents Association

Formed in 1963, the association was first known as the Harpeth Hall auxiliary and was composed of all the mothers of students. In 1964-66, Peggy Jones, mother of Nancy Jones Quillman ('67), was president of the auxiliary. Committee chairs included program, hospitality, nominating, telephone, publicity and directory. The directory chairman obtained the information about each family and typed the student directory for the school. Moreover, the parents maintained this responsibility over the next 25 years.

Past Presidents of the Parents Association

In the 1970s, a number of other events and committees evolved such as a father-daughter breakfast, new parents' night supper, a Many Lands Festival, a book fair, a parent/teacher lunch and a Grandmothers' Tea for Middle School students. Committee members added include cafeteria, graduation and art committee chairs. In 1981 during David Wood's term as headmaster, auxiliary meetings included a lunch with the teachers, the parents' night supper in the fall and a spring luncheon. In the same year, the Men's Club was formed because Mr. Wood wanted to encourage greater participation from fathers. The first president was David L. Ward.

Grandmothers Tea 1978

The 1980s saw increased expansion of the auxiliary with a grounds committee chairman, manpower chairman and a class mother coordinator for the Middle School as well as committees on cafeteria decoration and lunchroom programs. The school year 1983-84 marked the first Double Dip Raffle fund raiser, with Carol Rose (Mrs. Michael) and Mary Jane Smith (Mrs. Gilbert) as chairs. In 1985, the Round-Up replaced the Double Dip, with an country dinner, auction, raffle and dance on the campus. Faye Hale [Simpkins] and Mary

Myles Maille painting of Souby Hall auctioned at the 1999 Main Event, now hangs in Souby Hall.

Jane Smith (Mrs. Gilbert) were the first chairs. More than $20,000 was raised the first year and enabled the auxiliary to begin giving $10,000 annually for scholarship endowment.

In April 1990, the Main Event replaced the Round-Up; Donna Kestner (Mrs. Michael) and Nanci Barksdale (Mrs. Thomas) were chairs. The Main Event was designed to be a school community event and a more formal affair that included a seated dinner, dance, and live and silent auctions. The first event was held in a tent at Mary and David Proctor's home on Warner Place and is remembered as a sell-out in spite of a very cold night!

The impact of Leah Rhys' leadership began to be felt on the auxiliary in 1992. In 1992-1993, the men's club was combined with the auxiliary and the auxiliary's name was changed to the Harpeth Hall Parents Association Board. The booster club was started, and the bylaws, calendar, father-daughter banquet, Kirkman House and newsletter editor committees were added. In 1994-95 liaisons for new parents in both the Upper and Middle Schools were added, as well as senior parents after-prom party. In 1995-96, Davis-Kidd [bookstore] gift certificate sales began as a new fund raiser.

In Ann Teaff's first year as head of school (1997-98), a vice president of the Middle School was added to the executive committee, and a grocery store receipts committee was added as a new fund raiser. In 1998-99, the vice president of the parents network and vice president of campus activities were added to the executive committee, and ambassadors, book store volunteers, newsletter and receptions chairmen for the areas of art, choral/music, dance and drama committees were added. Parent ambassadors help with admission open houses and work with new families through a buddy system in order to "enhance the orientation of all new families," according to Lynn Ragland, president 1999-2000.

Father-Daughter Banquet on the General Jackson, 1991

'87 Round-Up pays off for Harpeth Hall

1987 Harpeth Hall fundraiser monies
went to the following:

Faculty enrichment	$5,000
Library	$4,000
Van	$10,000
Track and athletic complex	$15,000
English Department-Turnbull,	
Frontain	$1,350
Art Department-Goodwin-enlarger	$1,000
Drama Department-sound system	$2,743
Music Department	$1,500
Fine Arts Department-Matthews	
dance floor	$3,000
Latin Department-Farrand-films	$290
Science Department-chemistry-Norris	$1,440
(microscopes)	$386
French Department-Tuzeneu	$1,100
Math Department-Oxley	$795
Administration-Elaine Greene	$1,000
Leadership conference-Turnbull	$1,700
Middle School-furnishings for lobby	
Summer Enrichment-displays and	
representatives (MBA will participate)	$500
TOTAL	**$50,804**

By 1999, the Main Event fund raiser had evolved toward a school community gathering intended primarily to foster an *espirit d'corps* and, secondarily, to raise funds for the school. At that, it still is an effective event, raising more than $50,000 in recent years.

The parents association has steadily grown in function and volunteers. In 1997, Marguerite Wilson, 1997-99 president, reported that the association had "a record 320 families as members who helped with 420 volunteer opportunities with over 6,300 parent volunteer hours." In addition to that time commitment, the parents association raises meaningful money for the school—averaging more than $80,000 in recent years—and conducts meaningful supportive and enhancing roles for faculty and students alike. One of the most appreciated traditions is the annual Davis-Kidd gift certificate given to each faculty and staff member.

Monies raised are put to good uses—endowment funds and special gifts, as well as activities of the organization. Anne Whetsell, 1992-1993 president, feels that the parents association is a great organization. "Everyone involved has a real vested interest and everyone is enthusiastic. In addition, there is so much talent among the parents." Missy Rodriquez, 2000-2001 president, says that she has committed to such a large job because she believes in Harpeth Hall. "It is a strong school at a great point in its history. The girls become empowered here. It is rewarding to be a part of this school."

THE GOAL

In 1982-83, the purpose of the auxiliary was stated to be threefold: hospitality, aesthetic improvements of buildings and grounds and supplemental aid. In 1996 the purpose of the parents association was modified to the following statement: to foster communication within the parent body and with the administration and faculty and to sponsor many school events through volunteering and fund raising. Furthermore, it was emphasized that membership is voluntary. In 1997, the board of trustees set forth in its strategic plan that the goal of parent relationships is "to enhance the parent's involvement, trust, and support in all areas of school life."

Appendix

WARD–BELMONT MAY QUEENS
1922–1951

Sarah Morgan	1922
Florence Bell	1923
Marietta Moss	1925
Hope White	1926
Virginia Farmer	1927
Pauline McDonald	1928
Jean MacDonnell	1929
Isabelle Goodloe	1930
Grace Cavert	1931
Annie Kate Rebman	1932
Sarah Richardson	1933
Mary Elizabeth Polk	1934
Virginia Shaw	1935
Frances Prince	1936
Minnie Maude	1937
Sarah Logue	1938
Kathryne Walsh	1939
Kathryn Heitzberg	1940
Mary Elizabeth Masengill	1941
Dale Jellison	1942
Margie Eichenlaub	1943
Marnie Petrie	1944
Martha Maxwell Dickinson	1945
Joy Roberts	1946
Thelma Back	1947
Frances Purvis	1949
Kathryn Pankey	1950
Betsey Markley	1951

HARPETH HALL LADIES OF THE HALL
1952–2000

Donnie Berger	1952
Louise Bullard	1953
Martha Grizzard	1954
Rosalie Adams	1955
Carolyn Carmichael	1956
Linda Christie	1957
Evelyn Davis	1958
Betty Jane Guffee	1959
Kay Keeble	1960
Doris Matthews	1961
Judith Kinnard	1962
Pamela Polk	1963
Jacqueline Glover	1964
Caroline Phillips	1965
Carol Procter	1966
Melissa Burrus	1967
Tish Scott	1968
Barbara Meacham	1969
Karen Vaughn	1970
Beth Lewis	1971
Sabele Foster	1972
Susan Duvier	1973
Lee Ann Thornton	1974
Ellen Hobbs	1975
Susan Thornton	1976
Frances Diefendorf	1977
Amy Grant	1978
Susan Spickard	1979
Andree Akers	1980
Denise Smith	1981
Elizabeth Cochran	1982
Sarah W. Nichols	1983
Lillian Bradford	1984
Elizabeth Hightower	1985
Carol Cavin	1986
Susan Wattleworth	1987
Annis Marney	1988
Paige Ferragina	1989
Murray Polk	1990
Emily Haynes	1991
Carrie Crossman	1992
Kate Sherrard	1993
Holly Whetsell	1994
Katherine Wray	1995
Jennifer Kain	1996
Julia Brown	1997
Kate Celauro	1998
Lindsay Voigt	1999
Katie Hill	2000

HARPETH HALL HEADS OF SCHOOL

1951–1963	Susan Souby
1963–1979	Idanelle McMurry
1979–1980	Polly Fessey
1980–1991	David Wood
1991–1998	Leah Rhys
1998–present	Ann Teaff

HARPETH HALL FACULTY AND STAFF
1951–2001

Bettye Curry Abernathy
James Earl Adair
Karen G. Aid
Mia Alexander-Snow
Mary Lauren Barfield Allen*
Mary Prue Polk Alley
Rosalee Anderson
Jeannette S. Andrews
Brooks Appelbaum
Emma Jean Appleton
Mary Jane Pope Armfield
Leigh Zerfoss Atkins*
Jean Rose Ayers
Ann Bailey
Susan Litton Webster Bailey
Martha Ann Baird
Catherine Baker
Robert Baker
Judy Ballance
Mandy Simpson Barbara*
Sheila A. Barid
Betty Jane Guffee Barringer*
Vicki Hurd Bartholomew
Janet S. Barton
Tania Trotter Batson*
Susan McKeand Baughman*
Margaret Bean
Melisssa Bedinger-Hade
Jo Persels Benn
Robert Benson
Ray Berry
Mica Beyheimer
Dora S. Biegl
Kenneth Jeffrey Bilbrey
Susan Billings
Vera B. Binkley
Ann Blackburn
Louise Dortch Blair*
Diann Blakely
Kathryn Wesley Lazenby Boehm*
Elizabeth S. Boord
Robert J. Boudreau
Michael Wickham Bouton
James M. Bradfield
Lee Bradway
Cecil Brand
Katherine Brandon
Winnifred Breast
Carol C. Brewer
Mamie D. Brock
Vera Brooks
Hilrie Thompson Brown
Mary Brown
Susan Glasgow Brown*
Barbara Brummett
Emily Glasgow Bruno*
Elizabeth Sullins Buchweitz*
Marietta Eggleston Burleigh*
Marie F. Burr
Helen Burrus*
Rebecca R. Butler
Sharon Byers
Lane Weaver Byrd
Norman Richard Byrd
Roseann Caccioloa
Regina Calloway
Teresa Cameron
Clara Campbell
Patricia Gardner Campbell*
Barbara Carden
Patricia Reynolds Carney
Christine Lee Carpenter
Betty Holland Carr
Francis E. Carter III
David C. Cassel, Ph.D.
Patty L. Chadwell*
Stephen J. Chapman
Sharon Charney
Pickslay Cheek
Kathy L. Childress
Marees H. Choppin
Robert H. Christenberry
Nancy Christiansen
May Woodie Christopher
Merrie Morrissey Clark*
Isabelle Climer
Linda Lee Coker
Linda K. Colburn, Ph. D.
Rebecca Hiatt Collins
John Comfort
Molly Compton
Amy Conrad
Susan Cooney

James P. Cooper, Jr., Ph.D.
René D. Copeland
Marion Pickering Couch
Mary Springs Coutard
Tina Trinkler Cowlyn*
Jennifer A. Cox
David Crais
Ellen Crawford*
Pam D. Crawford
Cynthia Crenshaw
Lucinda J. Creswell
Denise L. Croker
Joseph P. Croker
Robbin L. Cross
Susan Copas Cundiff
Terry Currie
Marjorie Shaffer Dale*
Tiffany Gaston Dale*
Connally Davies*
Dugan Coughlan Davis
Dwana Davis
Josephine Davis
Leslie Patton Davis
Sandra Wagoner Davis
India Dennis
Lonita DesJardin
Kathryn King Dettwiller*
Tripp Tate Diedrichs
Catherine A. Dishman
Jan Johnston Dixon
Terry Smiley Dock
Molly Howell Dohrmann*
Anne Doolittle
Karen Douse
Phoebe B. Drews
Nancy White Duvier
Magdeline Dyer
Susie Dyer
Arthur R. Echerd, Jr., Ph.D.
Eleanor Eggleston
Sophronia Mayberry Eggleston
Danielle Guillot Eilender
Kyle Ann Ellis
Zita Elrod
Elizabeth Emerson
Elizabeth Pope Evans
Elinor Crawford Ewing
Frances Ewing*
Mark W. Fancher
Steve Farrand
Carolyn M. Felkel
Jane Grigor Ferrell

Polly Fessey*
Katherine Kennedy Flouhouse*
Felix Fly
Jennifer Ford
Elizabeth Anne Salem Foster
McLauren P. Foster
Lucy Fountain
Varina Frazer
Lonnie Frey
Gerald D. Fridrich, Jr.
Patricia Frontain
Raymond Jean Frontain, Ph.D.
Emily Bivens Fuller
Donna Kaye Fulton
Cathey Fuqua
Virginia Galgano
Ginny M. Garrison
William Gehrese
Alice M. Gericke
Lillian Roe Gilmer*
Judith Scot-Smith Girgus
Elizabeth Henig Glenn
Elizabeth Spencer Goldman
Michael Goodwin
Peter Goodwin
Dona Gower, Ph.D.
Martha Stewart Grace
Hila Murchison Graham
Sally Graham, Ph.D.
Lori C. Graves
Nancy Gray, Ph.D.
Virginia Gray
Elizabeth S. Greathouse
Elaine Green
Martha Corwin Gregory
Karl E. Grier
Dorothea Griffin
Nancy Guerard Grimes
Jane Linebaugh Groos*
Landis Shaw Gullett*
Melissa Hade
Julie H. Haffner
Carole C. Hagan
Linda Jones Hall
Jaqueline Haloua-Dismukes
Stephanie S. Hamilton
Martha Overholser Hammonds
Jessie Harbison
Laetitia Wenning Hardin*
Margaret L. Harmon
Brooks Harris
Renita Hartsock

Ida Hawkins
Jane VandeRoovaart Haynes
Laura Hays
William B. Hayward
John F. Hazen
Jack Henderson, Ph.D.
Nan Henig
Janet Hensley
Mary Russell Robinson Herod
Peggy Herring
Melinda A. Higgins
Doris Hill
Jess Baumhauer Hill
Andi Boklage Holbrook*
Patricia Hollingsworth
Penelope Lee Homan
Philip A. Hooper
Jean Martin Hoover
John S. Hopple, Ph.D.
Ginger R. Horton
Joan Howard
Ruth Hoffman Howard
Therese Howell
Betty Huesmann
Laura Huff
Marilyn Boggs Hunter
Peter J. Iano, Ph.D.
Jane Berry Jacques*
Margaret Russ Jeffords*
Blair Jenkins
Tommy Jenkins
Sheila Johansson
Joanna Thornton Johnson
Judy C. Johnson
A. Heath Jones III
Deborah Jones
Dorothy Jones
Frank Jones
Gloria Jones
Kristen A. Jones
Mary Evelyn Jones
Barbara Jordan
Curtis Jordan
Driver Joslin
Laura E. G. Joyner
Rita E. Kaplan
Linda D. Karwedsky
Majorie Kastrinsky
Angela Keith
Susan Roberts Kennedy
Sandra Keys
Suzanne Killmer

Tracy Kimberlin
Charles E. Kimbro
Anne Keen King
Elizabeth Waits King
Paul Kingsbury
Stacy Stansell Klein, Ph.D.
Janette Fox Klocko
Anissa Konieczny
Steven C. Kramer
Ethel Krasney
Georgianne Moran Kruklinski*
Billie Pyle Kuykendall
Lisa Eveleigh Kyriakoudes
Luann Evans Landon
William Lauderdale, Jr.
Joyce Lee
Lisa Lee*
Sally Uptegrove Lee
Liza Beazley Lentz
Malka Levran
Leslie Lanalee Lewis
Margaret Libby
Polly L. Linden
Lenore Litkenhous
Dana B. Long-Innes
Judy Lowe
Michael Lowry
Sally Snell Mabry
Jane Capps Macey*
Robert MacLamore
Mary Victoria MacLean
Betsy Bugg Malone
Elizabeth Marshall
Mary Lee Mathews
    Manier, Ph.D.*
Ruth McMurtrey Mann
Nancy Jane Manning
Dan Ellen Brock Maples
Betty Marney, Ph.D.
Elizabeth Marshall
Margie Fish Martin*
Paula Martin
Leslie Matthews
Marie Dodson Maxwell*
Marisa Ortega Mayhan
Margha McCarthy
Lynn Maddox McDonald
Lucile Drain McLean
Susan Ralston McLean*
Donald McMahan
Peggy McMurray*
Idanelle McMurry*

Colene Meier
Jacqueline Milam
Cynthia Miller
Lilborune I. Mills, Ph.D.
Catherine Puryear Mims
Ella Puryear Mims*
Jeff K. Minikus
Rev. Henry Peter Minton, Jr.
Joyce Lehman Minton
Susan Gay Mitchell
Victoria M. Moats
Donna Olson Montague
Tracy Wright Moor
Katherine Moore
Mildred B. Moore
Pat Neblett Moran*
Sachiko Morrey
Louise Douglas Morrison, Ph.D.*
Debra Morton
Kathy Thweatt Morton*
Penelope Mountfort
La-Voe Mulgrew
Marilyn Musterman
Derah Houseworth Myers, Ph.D.
Kristina Muth Myrick
M. Scott Myrick
Karen Rom Nash
Elizabeth Neale
Penelope Neale
Betty Latham Nelson*
Vernon M. Nelson
Polly Jordan Nichols*
Emily Noel*
Jane Spotts Norris
Kay Fossick Norton
Sallie King Norton*
Megan O'Brien
Jacqueline O'Keefe
Genella Olker
Susan O'Neal
Ginger Osborn*
Katharine B. Oser
Margaret Henry Ottarson
Carol C. Oxley
Alison Pagliara
Ophelia Thompson Paine*
Karen Painter
Natalie A. Panshin
Betty Parham
Cynthia Parker
Kay L. Parker
Lucinda Parker*

Madeline Blackman Parker*
Robert Parsons, Ph.D.
Betty Partee
Rosemary Souter Paschall
Marilee Patnode
Louise C. W. Patton
German A. Pavia
Margaret Peeler
Phyllis T. Pennington
Willie Perry
Thad Persons
Ann Puckett Petersen
Chantal Philippon-Daniel
Hilary Reneé Pick
Muffet Pickel
Jennifer Pledger
Mary McCrory Plummer
Linda Kay Poag
Judy Jones Pointer
Carlyn Grau Poole
Paul A. Poropatic
Laurie Postlewate
Ann C. Poteet
Kathy Powell
Linda K. Prestidge
Mary Lou Primm
Clay Pullias
Erika Radtke
Susan Ralston
D. J. Ranta
Mary McMillan Rasmussen
Darrell Ray
Nancy E. Reed
Lucy Reese
Margaret E. Renkl
Claire Craig Reynolds
Anna Rhone
Leah Schwantes Rhys
Lisa Rice
Charles S. Riddle III
Kay Riddle
Susan Nussbaum Rieder
Kathryn Sue Ritchie
Karen Roark
Caroline Isbell Roberts
Eleanor Flautt Roberts
Mary M. Roberts
Peggy Foutch Robinson
Ruth Rodgers
Margaret Ross, Ph.D.
Marian Henry Ross
Lynne Rothrock

Frances Roy, Ph.D.*
Barbara Wallace Royse*
Nancy Sherman Rumsey
Susan Kaufman Russ
Nan Norman Russell
Kris Ruswick
Joanna Rutter
Ann Edmondson Sanders
Lindy Beazley Sayers
Lisa Griffin Schatz*
Mary Taylor Schell
Stephanie A. Schlanger
Anita Woodcock Schmid*
Joan Schmitt
Bonnie Daryl Schulkin
Karen T. Schwartz
Amy Sebes
Martha Wilkinson Sedgwick
Nancy Dwight Seiters
L. George Sellers
Murray McCowen Sellers, Ph.D.
Patricia Settle*
Dolores Ann Shaw
Stephanie Sheahan
Richie Simmons
Elaine Simpson
Emily Skaggs
Georgia Slupe
Dorothy Martin Smith
Lee Marshal Smith
Rena Smith
Tracy Smith
Margaret Walker Smithey
Susan Souby
Marilee Spain
Meredith Ann Sparks
Lisa Ferguson Springman*
Tony Springman
Laura Squyres
Amy L. Stallings
Sarah Frost Stamps
Bonita Zola Steele
Elizabeth Stelling
Lillian Campbell Stewart*
Jane Gwinn Stumpf*
Kerry Sullivan
Sandra Sullivan
Laura Lynn Svaren
Earlon Swancy
Joyce Szabo
Nora Tatum
Elizabeth F. Taylor

Ann M. Teaff
Madeline Terry
Nancye Thomas, Ph.D.
Coby Thompson
Helen Hartsook Thompson
Mary Britton Thompson*
Kate Wallis Thweatt*
Fred L. Tindall
Annie Orr Trost*
Susan Trzuskowski
Betsy Turnbull
Rev. Gordon Turnbull
Dee Dee Turner
Warren Turner, Ph.D.
Paul-Leon Tuzeneu
Masami Izumida Tyson
James Dautzler Umbarger
Brad J. Ungurait
Frederique Vallord
Robert R. Van Cleave
Germaine VanCleemput
Colene Meier VanDeusen
Jesse VanVolkenburgh
Legare Davis Vest
Catarina Andrea Vietorisz
Nancy Jane Vining
Rose Vinson
Anne Abernathy Wade
Ingelein Smith Walker*
Susan Woodward Walker
Judith Elaine Wall
Timothy Michael Wallace
Caroline Hilton Ward*
Joyce Crutcher Ward*
James I. Warren
Joan Metz Warterfield
Mary Watkins Wasik
Nina Watkins
Violet Jane Watkins
Lydia A. Watt
Mark Webb
Tad Wert
Patricia Whitehurst
Katherine A. Wieczerza
Roberta Sue Wikle
Dianne Buttrey Wild*
Brad Williams
Elizabeth Herbert Williams
Juanita Greene Williams
Margaret Lauderdale Williams*
Dorothy Jones Willis
Louise Parker Wills

Alma Wilson
Susan Hynds Wingler
Catharine Winnia
Charles Witherspoon
Gail Wolery
David E. Wood, Sr.
Suzanne Macksound Wooten
Aaron C. Wynn
Frances E. Wynne
Betty Yazagaray
Joelyn Yoder
Judith Gaines Young
Thomas Daniel Young, Ph.D.
Pamela Yount
Wendy Lawrence Zerface*
Jeanne Pilkerton Zerfoss*

List includes faculty and staff who have worked at Harpeth Hall for one or more years.
* indicates alumnae

CHAIRS OF THE
BOARD OF TRUSTEES

1951–1955	William Waller
1956–1977	Daugh W. Smith
1977–1981	John S. Beasley II
1981–1983	Jeanne Pilkerton Zerfoss (W-B '43)
1983–1987	Robert W. Kitchel
1987–1989	Mary Schlater Stumb ('53)
1989–1991	Richard W. Oliver, Ph.D.
1991–1995	Peggy Smith Warner ('54)
1995–1998	Robert C. Hilton
1998–2000	Carol Clark Elam ('66)

HONORARY TRUSTEES

Mandy Simpson Barbara ('54) (*inactive*)
Melinda Owen Bass ('58)
Martin S. Brown, Sr.
Linda Williams Dale ('56)
Patricia C. Frist
Robert W. Kitchel
Idanelle McMurry (W-B '43)
Britton H. Nielsen
Richard W. Oliver, Ph.D.
Eugene Pargh
Barbara Massey Rogers ('56)
W. Lucas Simons
Mary Schlater Stumb ('53)
Peggy Smith Warner ('54)

PRESIDENTS OF THE
ALUMNAE ASSOCIATION

1964–1974	Linda Williams Dale	('56)
1974–1976	Patsy White Bradshaw	('59)
1976–1978	Alva Herbert Wilk	('59)
1978–1980	Carolyn Russell	('64)
1980–1982	Beth Creighton Harwell	('55)
1982–1984	Carole Minton Nelson	('56)
1984–1986	Gray Oliver Thornburg	('72)
1986–1988	Mary Jo Freeman Johnson	('73)
1988–1990	Beth Lewis Murphy	('71)
1990–1991	Jane Mabry Jackson	('82)
1991–1993	Beth Thornton Rader	('82)
1993–1994	Nancy Graves Beveridge	('80)
1994–1995	Josephine Kelley Darwin	('73)
1995–1996	Tina Cummings Huggins	('69)
1996–1997	Nancy Short Phipps	('75)
1997–1998	Emily Cate Tidwell	('75)
1998–1999	Cathy Petway Shull	('64)
1999–2000	Emily Perkins Zerfoss	('75)
2000–2001	Sarah Winn Nichols	('83)

PRESIDENTS OF THE
PARENTS AUXILIARY

1965–1966	Peggy Jones (Mrs. Robert L. Jr.)
1966–1967	Jeanne Pilkerton Zerfoss (Mrs. Thomas B. Jr.) (W-B '43)
1967–1968	Keith Lauderdale (Mrs. W.A.)
1968–1969	Kitty Patrick (Mrs. R.C. Jr.)
1969–1970	Dot Woods (Mrs. DeVaughn)
1970–1971	Susan White Perry (Mrs. J.L. Jr.)
1971–1972	Gloria Grant (Mrs. Burton P.)
1972–1973	Louise Armistead Martin (Mrs. Joseph Jr.) (W-B '47)
1973–1974	Cecy Reed (Mrs. James H. III)
1974–1975	Carolyn Bass Cate (Mrs. George H. Jr.) (W-B '49)
1975–1976	Alice Casey Mathews (Mrs. Robert C. Jr.) (W-B '49)
1976–1977	Dean Gillespie Reeves (Mrs. Robert L.) ('53)
1977–1978	Dean Gillespie Reeves (Mrs. Robert L.) ('53)
1978–1979	Anne Shockley (Mrs. John R.)
1979–1980	Virginia Sullivan (Mrs. Richard H.)
1980–1981	Melissa Luton Bradford (Mrs. William H.) ('55)
1981–1982	Alva Herbert Wilk (Mrs. Frank A. Jr.) ('59)

1982–1983	Sandra Polk (Mrs. Marshall III)
1983–1984	Kay Williams (Mrs. Jack)
1984–1985	Britton Nielsen (Mrs. Norris)
1985–1986	Sandra Gardner (Mrs. Carl A.)
1986–1987	Mary Jane Smith (Mrs. Gilbert)
1987–1988	Nancy Johnston (Mrs. Donald)
1988–1989	Sallie Bailey (Mrs. John)
1989–1990	Peggy Stanford Palmer (Mrs. Joe) ('62)
1990–1991	Sherri Chilton (Mrs. Robert)
1991–1992	Nanci Barksdale (Mrs. Thomas)
1992–1993	Anne Whetsell (Mrs. William Jr)
1993–1994	Lynn Terry (Mrs. Richard)
1994–1995	Mary Cummings (Mrs. Greer)
1995–1996	Judy Haury (Mrs. Sandy)
1996–1997	Elaine Jackson (Mrs. Andrew)
1997–1999	Marguerite Wilson (Mrs. John R.)
1999–2000	Lynn Ragland (Mrs. James B. Jr.)
2000–2001	Missy Rodriquez (Mrs. Michael)

Index

Accreditation 48
Allison, Annie C. 22
Allison, Annie C., Library 64, **73**, 75, 76, 85
Alma Mater 51
Alumnae association 140-147
    activities 142-145
    Annual Giving Program 141
    Distinguished Alumna
        Award 146-147
    Hallways 52
    presidents 157
    reunions 144-145
    reunion song 144
American Field Service 93
Arts 105, 134-135
Athletics 56, **65**, 87-89, 108-110,
    132-133
Awards
    Awards Day 113
    Cindy Crist Art Purchase 117, 135
    Citizenship 58
    Dede Bullard Wallace 58, 85, 93
    Distinguished Alumna 146-147
    Elizabeth Pope Evans 104
    Emmons Woolwine 110
    Katie Wray 58, 70, 113

Bear Lair 100, 103, 120
Belmont College 14-18
    campus 16, **20**
    curriculum 17
    customs and regulations 18
    founders 14-15
Board of trustees 148-150,
    chairs 157
    charter members 39

honorary 157
    national advisory council 150
Bullard, Dede 58
Bullard, Ella Petway and George N.,
    Center for Student Activities 120
Bullard Gymnasium **44**, 56, 85, 120

Carell, Ann Scott, Library 121
Carell Visiting Artist and Writer Series 135
Chadwell, Patty 44-45
Chadwell, Patty, Tennis Courts 101
Clubs 47, **82**, 114, 116, 130, 131
    Beyond Hate 124, 131
    dance 86, 105
    debate 117
    fair 114, 116
    glee 67, 79
    Key 103, 114, 116, 130
    outing 116
    pep 131
    picnic 67, 112-113
    Playmakers 131, 134
    Quill & Scroll 114
    school clubs
        changes 112
        origins 46
        songs 66
    Spanish **59**
    Ward-Belmont 26-27
College tours 103, 107, 121
Community Service Day 130
Crist, Cindy, Art Collection and Art
    Purchase Award 117
Cubby Hole 71
Cum Laude Society 83
Curb Music Center 120

Dance program 86, **99**, 105, 134-135
Dances 94, 110
    combos 64-65
    proms 113, 130
    tea dance 57, **59**, 64-65
Davis, Frances Bond, Auditorium 85
Davis, Frances Bond, Theatre 126
Distinguished Alumna Award 146-147

Ellis Art Studio 121

Faculty 154-157
    Appreciation Day 102
    original 41
Father-Daughter Banquet 103, 113, **152**
Fessy, Polly 90
Frist, Dorothy Cate, Hall 101

George Washington Birthday
    Celebration 54, **70**, **81**, 96, **97**, 112, 130
Graduation 50, **51**, **62**, **77**, 111

Habitat for Humanity 130
Hallmarks 135
Halloween Carnival 130, **143**
Hallways 52
Heads of School 154
    Polly Fessey 90
    Idanelle McMurry 64, 72, 73, 74-76, **77**,
        93, 139
    Leah Rhys 122-124
    Susan Souby 38-42, 48-49, 74
    Ann Teaff 125-126, 137
    David Wood 102-103, 121
Heron, Miss Susan 14
Honor Council 115

Honor Society 66, 70
Hood, Miss Ida 14
Horton, Leigh, Garden 101

Ingram Dining Hall 120

Junior-Senior Day 68, 96

Kirkman House 11, 55, 121

Lady of the Hall 52, 70, 113, 130, 154
Little Harpeth 39, 45, 100

Magnolia 52
Massey, Jack C., Center for Mathematics
    and Science 100, **120**, 121
May Queens 154
McMurry Center for Arts and Athletics 85
McMurry, Idanelle 64, 72, 73, 74-76, **77**,
    93, 139
Melkus Science Center 120
Men's club 102, 113
Milestones 23, 47, 50, 62, 70, 97, 117
Mole Run 43, 71
Morehead Scholarship 103
Morrison, Catherine E. 24
Morrison, Catherine E., Gymnasium 85
Motto 52

National Merit Scholars 72, 107
Nichols, Polly Jordan 141

Opening 42-44
Organization of Harpeth Hall 37-42

Parents association 151-153
    presidents 157
Penstaff 94
Plays 50, 68-69, 86, 103, 115, 135
Pledge 53, 73
Presidential Scholars 136
Purchase of property 38

Retreats 114
Reunions 33, 144-145
Rhys, Leah 122-124

Seal 52, back cover
Senior House 42, **55**, 72-73, 96, 126
Senior Recognition Day 113
Sheridan, Marnie, Gallery 85, 126
Smith, Daugh W. 37, **38**, **76**, 85
    Memorial Garden 85
    Middle School 84, 85, 90, 124
        founding 90
        grades added 101, 124
        Honor Day 111
Souby Hall **38**, 42, **73**, 100, cover,
    jacket flap
Souby, Susan S. 38-42, 48-49, 74
Step Singing 53, 111
Student council 47, 71, 89, 94, 110
Stump 71

Teaff, Ann 125-126, 137

Uniforms 83, 114

Wallace, Dede Bullard, Award 58, 85, 93
Wallace, Louise Bullard, Educational Wing 85
Ward-Belmont 18-35
    accreditation 20
    activities **19**, 23-28
    campus 22-23
    clubs 26-27
    curriculum 19-21
    demise 30-35
    George Washington Birthday
        Celebration 29, **32**
    Little School 22
    May Day and May Queen 28-29, 154
    presidents 19
    publications 23
    regulations for day students 21
    reunion 33
    special events 28-29
Ward-Belmont Room 100
Ward Seminary 10-13
    curriculum 10, 12-13
    founders 10
    location 11
    motto 12
    presidents 13
    reputation 12-13
Winterim 75, 84, 106, **127**
Wood, David 102-103, 121
Wray, Ellen Kathleen (Katie) 58, 70

*Numerical entries in bold-faced type
refer to photographs.*